A Good Crew Is Hard to Find

BY THE SAME AUTHOR

The Cruise of the *Jest*
The Good Sailor

A Good Crew
Is Hard to Find

Jon Adams

Slack Water Press

Slack Water Press, Mill Valley 94941

Copyright © 2024 Jon Adams
All rights reserved

ISBN 978-0-9797613-8-6

A Green Book: The paper used in this publication
meets standards for sustainable forestry.

for Franziska

					Soon as the king
saw Jason, he was sure he was the man
and right away contrived a labor for him,
a cruel voyage, in the hope that he
would die at sea or fighting savages
and never make the journey home to Greece.

                Apollonius of Rhodes, *Argonautica*

Contents

Selene 3

Gloria Fontaine 73

Stella Maris 145

Selene

THE RAIN HAS STOPPED and the sun shines bright and harsh on Kallang Basin while to the northwest heavy clouds still hang above Singapore. Jamie stands in the cockpit of the ketch *Selene* as the sun steams the moisture off the deck. The air is heavy and windless, humidity in the eighties. To the north brown water flows out of the Kallang River, carrying debris into the basin where the ketch lies at anchor. The debris swirls around the anchor chain as it slowly passes the ketch on the outgoing tide. Eventually it will find its way out to sea where everything drifts apart.

The sound of voices carries across the water. Jamie looks over at the sloop *Sundowner* as the Kepplers climb in their dinghy and row to the boat club. Debora isn't with them. Then Meg shouts from the saloon, "Jamie, get the dinghy ready, we're going ashore." He unties the painter and brings the dinghy alongside the ketch. Meg and Kate climb on deck, both attractive in their shore clothes, pastel blouses, knee-length shorts and sandals. Jamie holds the dinghy steady as they climb in, Meg in the bow and Kate in the stern. He rows across the basin, past *Sundowner,* and up to the boat-club landing. He ships his inboard oar and looks off at *Sundowner*. "Jamie, stop mooning and hold the dinghy steady so we can get out." He grabs the landing as Meg climbs out. She always pushes off with her back foot, driving the bow of the dinghy away from the landing.

Kate climbs out. "We'll be back in time for dinner. So have something ready." They walk through the boat club, two women in their mid-thirties, more than ten years older than he is. He waits until they disappear up the old airport road and then he starts rowing back toward *Selene.* Before he reaches the ketch, Debora calls to him. "Jamie! Jaaamieee!" He stops rowing for a moment and then swings the dinghy around and heads toward *Sundowner*. He climbs aboard the sloop and ties the dinghy aft. Debora has gone below and as he climbs down the companionway she has already taken off her blouse.

"Debbie . . . what did you tell your parents?"

"I said I had a headache."

Selene

He leans in and kisses her forehead. "How is it now?"

She laughs and yanks his t-shirt over his head and pushes him on the settee and then she pulls down his shorts and climbs on top of him.

Later Jamie rows Debora to the boat club. There aren't any people at the club, there aren't even any boats. There's just a sign and showers with sun-warmed water. They take a shower together, soaping each other. The shower is too intimate for talking, letting them put off saying good-bye to each other. Jamie rows Debora back to *Sundowner* and she climbs aboard. "We'll be leaving Singapore soon."

"Yes. We are too. We'll see each other in Penang."

Debora holds on to a shroud and leans over him. "What if we miss each other there?"

"We won't. Everyone stops in Penang. It's the last port before crossing the Indian Ocean."

"I think my parents want to go to India."

"Anyone can go to India. Tell you parents to go to the Seychelles."

"Why? What's in the Seychelles?"

"There's a schooner there, *Stella Maris*. I'm going to join her."

Jamie is in the galley washing up the dinner dishes when Debora calls, "Ahoy, *Selene!*"

Meg yells from the saloon, "Jamie, that sounds like that little bitch from *Sundowner*. Go see what she wants."

Jamie walks through the saloon where Meg and Kate are sitting across from each other, smoking their after-dinner cigarettes. He climbs up to the cockpit and looks over the side. Debora is sitting in the dinghy wearing a cream blouse and dark brown shorts.

"Hi, Debbie."

"Jamie, come with me for a walk." He climbs in the dinghy and she starts for the boat-club landing.

"That's a nice blouse. It looks expensive."

"It's silk. My father bought it for me."

He watches her straining at the oars. "Let me row. We can go up the river."

"No, I want to go ashore. I want to walk." Her rowing is erratic and with the last pull of the oars she rams the dinghy into the landing.

"That wasn't very handsome."

"Handsome is as handsome does. So now you know how I feel."

They stand facing each other. "What do you want me to do?"

Selene

She turns and walks out to the old airport road. "You could ask my parents to join *Sundowner*."

He walks a few steps behind. "You know your parents don't like me, especially your mother."

She turns to him. "My mother knocks everyone. She thinks you are immature because you haven't done anything yet."

"She sounds like my uncle. *Go to sea. If you stay at home you'll never amount to anything.*"

"My father likes you. He can teach you how to sail. Then you can be something more than a cook."

"I already told Meg and Kate I would watch *Selene* in Port Swettenham so they can visit Kuala Lumpur for a few days." She turns away again and walks up the road. "Wait, Debbie." He reaches for her shoulder and feels the warm silk. "I'll ask your father in Penang, how's that?"

She turns back. "You promise?"

"I promise."

She kisses him. When she breaks away she looks off toward the city. "There. Look at the glow from the lights above Singapore. They are my witness, a promise made in heaven." She laughs and takes his hand. "Let's walk along the waterfront."

"How far do you want to walk?"

"I want to walk until there's no more walking."

A Good Crew Is Hard to Find

The galley on *Selene* is forward of the mainmast with a bulkhead separating it from the saloon. Jamie stands in the galley eating because Meg and Kate are in the saloon lighting up their after-breakfast cigarettes. Meg yells, "Jamie, bring some more coffee." Jamie puts down his plate next to the sink, picks up the coffee pot and a cup and carries them into the saloon. He fills their cups and then pours himself a cup.

Meg blows smoke at him. "You say good-bye to that Keppler girl last night? A good-looking guy like you, you need to watch out for young things like her. They don't know what they want, so they want everything."

Jamie smiles. "I never know what women want." He walks back to the galley.

Meg stops him. "Go get the dinghy ready. We're going ashore in a minute.

"Are you going shopping again?"

Meg blows more smoke. "It's none of your business what we do."

Kate looks at Meg. "Don't be so snarky." She turns to Jamie. "We need to order supplies and fuel. We're leaving Singapore in a day or two." She turns back to Meg. "Is it okay if I tell him that?"

"You can tell him to kiss my ass for all I care."

Selene

Jamie drops Meg and Kate off at the boat-club landing and returns to *Selene*. He warms up his coffee and takes it on deck. Brown water swirls around the ketch, carrying debris back into the basin with the incoming tide. *Sundowner* is gone and there are no other boats in the basin. Jamie finishes his coffee and is about to go below and wash up the breakfast dishes when he sees a sailboat entering the basin with her sails filling and collapsing in the light air. The tide is about to turn and without an engine the boat won't make it to the anchorage. Jamie climbs in the dinghy and rows down the basin. "Throw me a line and I'll tow you in." The man on the sailboat gets a line ready and hands it down and Jamie begins rowing up the basin, sweating in the morning sun. When the man releases his anchor Jamie unties the towline and rows alongside the boat. "Mind if I come aboard?" The man stops coiling the towline and waves him toward the cockpit.

They sit in the cockpit facing each other, a young man, tanned and blonde and an older man, weathered and gray.

"You don't have an engine?"

The man points with a long finger. "My spar deck." Jamie looks at the wooden mast and booms lashed on deck.

"Where did you sail from?"

"Do you talk to fish?"

"No, I haven't tried that. Do the fish talk?"

"No, fish can't talk. There was a fish in the Java Sea. He came most days and I talked to him. Have you found Michael and Gary yet?"

"No, I don't know any Michael and Gary."

The man points to *Selene*. "That's Michael and Gary's boat."

"I don't think so. *Selene* belongs to Meg and Kate, Meg Green and Kate Henderson. You must be thinking of some other *Selene*.

"Women are a curse at sea."

"I don't know about that. I've been on *Selene* since Suva. That's where I joined her. Meg and Kate do all the sailing. I think they are pretty good at it. I'm just the cook."

"Someone should find Michael and Gary. You will do that."

"Do you think they disappeared?"

"They didn't disappear. Something happened to them." He points to *Selene* again. "Look for them there."

Jamie hears Meg hailing him from the boat-club landing. "I have to shove off. Maybe we can talk again sometime." He stands up and unties his dinghy.

Selene

"We will talk again soon."

Jamie climbs in his dinghy and rows around the stern of the boat. *Dodona*, Plymouth.

Meg and Kate climb aboard *Selene* and Jamie goes in the galley and starts cleaning up. Meg and Kate sit in the saloon and light up cigarettes. He hears them arguing in whispers. "Jamie, come here." Jamie goes in the saloon. "What were you talking to Captain Waters about?"

"Is that his name? I couldn't get much out of him. He says he talks to fish. Other than that, he speaks in riddles."

Kate laughs. "Yes, he acts like he can tell the future, like some soothsayer or something."

Meg stares at Jamie. "He's a crazy old man who sails alone. They say this is his fifth voyage around the world and he probably gets crazier each time. You should stay away from him."

Jamie is still cleaning up the galley when Meg and Kate finish their after-breakfast cigarettes and get *Selene* underway. Kate starts the engine and stands by the helm as Meg raises the anchor. When he is finished in the galley, Jamie pokes his head out the companionway hatch. Kate is bringing the ketch up to the fuel dock and without looking at him she tells him to get the stern line. Meg hops ashore and uses the bow line to snub the ketch and bring her to a stop alongside the dock. Jamie steps ashore and starts to tie the stern line to a cleat when Kate tells him to double-up the line. "We'll be getting underway soon."

Meg takes the diesel nozzle and starts filling the fuel tank and Kate starts filling the water tank, using a nylon stocking as a filter. A delivery truck arrives and Jamie carries the supplies aboard and then below. Potatoes, onions, pasta, flour, powdered milk, jam, twelve dozen eggs, and cans of fruit and vegetables. Jamie is still storing everything when a car arrives with covered dishes of food, a present from Mr. Wong. Meg and Kate met Mr. Wong in a restaurant and Mr. Wong invited them to join him in a private room. The lunch in the private room turned into a party that lasted most of the afternoon, and afterwards Mr. Wong invited them to visit him in Kuala Lumpur.

The day is overcast and windless. Meg and Kate haven't set the watch yet and both sit in the shade of the sailing awning as Kate powers the ketch up the Malacca Strait. Jamie serves lunch in the cockpit with the food Mr. Wong sent. He sets up the cockpit table

Selene

and then brings up a platter with dishes of beef and green beans, chicken with rice, and skewered grilled meat.

"Jamie, takes these chopsticks away and bring some forks, for chrissakes."

"Jamie, squeeze some lime in a pitcher of water and bring it up too."

"You don't want a beer? Mr. Wong sent two cases of Tiger."

"We don't drink at sea. We told you that before and you would remember it if you didn't walk around with your head where it doesn't belong. Go get the forks and water."

Jamie sits in the companionway looking at the night. There is little to see, no horizon or stars, just the lights of the ships passing farther out in the Strait. Meg is at the helm. She lights a cigarette and the flame of the match points aft. "Hit the sack, Jamie. I want coffee at six in the morning." Jamie walks through the saloon. With the engine running it's too hot to sleep aft and Kate is in one of the bunks above the settee. Jamie continues through the galley to his bunk in the forepeak. He didn't do much during the day but leaving port has worn him out. He climbs in his bunk and falls asleep.

A Good Crew Is Hard to Find

Sometime during the night Kate visits him. She climbs in his bunk, pulls his shorts down and lowers herself on top of him. The smell of her cigarette breath is heavy in his face. She doesn't make any noise and the bunk doesn't creak. When she is finished she tells him not to tell Meg. She always says that. Meg too. Meg says not to tell Kate. He knows they both know what goes on but he thinks they pretend not to know because if it's a secret then they don't have to talk about it. They never visit him in port, only at sea when one of them has the watch. He wishes they didn't smoke.

There is still no wind as Kate heads *Selene* up the Strait. They hug the Malaysian coast while Sumatra is hidden in the haze off to port. Jamie prepares lunch, the last of the food Mr. Wong sent.

"Jamie, go wake up Meg. It's time for her watch."

"You do it. She's too snappish when she wakes up. I'll take the helm." Kate goes below and Jamie hears some complaining, the heat, the lack of wind, the noise of the engine. They were in Singapore too long and the women haven't adjusted yet to standing watch-and-watch. They all sit together in the cockpit. Meg steers with her bare foot on the helm as she eats a plate of fried noodles with a fork.

Selene

"Jamie, go get the salt."

"You don't put salt on Chinese food. If you want to talk to Kate alone, wait until I go do the washing up."

"Since when do you start talking back?"

Jamie smiles. "I think what we need is something sweet. How about if I make an apple cake?"

The women are pleased but they don't say anything. Kate goes below to write the log and Jamie carries the empty plates to the galley and washes up. He remembers that there aren't any apples but there are some mangoes. He makes a simple cake batter and puts mango wedges in it and serves it with coffee at four o'clock. Meg and Kate eat the entire cake and afterwards they don't want any dinner. Jamie stands in the galley eating fried eggs, staring at the bulkhead.

In the late afternoon they enter the passage between the islands that leads to Port Swettenham. There's a heavy smell in the air, rotting vegetation, raw sewage, crowded humanity, he can't tell. The smell slowly dissipates as the islands fall away, revealing a wide harbor.

As soon as they tie up to a wharf, Meg and Kate hurry off with overnight bags to look for a taxi to take them to Kuala Lumpur. Jamie finds a hose on the wharf and washes down the deck of the ketch and then he stands on the wharf and uses the hose to take a shower. He goes in the galley and looks at the twelve dozen eggs. He lights the stove and puts on a pan of water and then one by one dips the eggs in boiling water for five seconds. It's dark by the time he has sealed all the eggs. He breaks open a case of beer and takes a bottle aft to the navigation table and turns on the shortwave radio, something Meg has forbidden him to do. He sips the beer and stares at the navigation table, then he puts the beer down and pulls out the drawer under the table and takes out the logbook. He reads the first entry. *Anchored at Bora Bora 15:00. After clearing with the French officials, moved to the quay at Vaitape.* He looks in the drawer and finds a small brown bottle without a label. The cap of the bottle has an eyedropper and he lets it drip on a sheet of plotting paper. The liquid looks oily and it has a faint smell of dirty socks. He holds the bottle up to the light. Half full. He puts the bottle and logbook back and closes the drawer. He sits in the companionway hatch drinking beer, barely listening to the announcer on radio talking about Soviet missiles in Cuba and the Americans threatening to quarantine the island. The night is starless and the tide gently rocks the ketch against the wharf.

Selene

In the morning *Dodona* is anchored in the harbor. Jamie eats fried eggs and drinks a cup of coffee in the cockpit. He uses the main halyard to lower the dinghy over the side and rows over to *Dodona*. As he comes alongside he ships his oars and Captain Waters waves him aboard. They sit in the cockpit opposite each other. "You said we would meet again."

"You haven't found Michael and Gary."

"Not yet. I read *Selene's* logbook. It begins in Bora Bora. There's no logbook before that, nothing from San Diego to Bora Bora. Do you know why? Did something happen before Bora Bora?"

Captain Waters stares at Jamie. "I will tell you. It was in Papeete. Tahitian women came and took Michael and Gary away, to the other side of the island. They were gone a long time."

Jamie heard that Tahitian women were irresistible. "What did Meg and Kate do?"

"They tried to leave Papeete. They tried to sail away without Michael and Gary. The French didn't like that. They don't want men marooned on their island. The French brought Michael and Gary back to Papeete and told them to leave. Four sailed from Tahiti, only two arrived in Bora Bora."

"What happened to Michael and Gary?

"Mutiny is a terrible crime."

"Do you think they were poisoned?"

"Why use poison when you can use an ocean?"

Jamie looks off at the clouds piling up over the Strait. It will rain later in the day. "You think they threw the men overboard."

"Make them confess. You will do this."

"I don't know. I have to think about it."

"You do not have a choice."

Jamie returns to *Selene* and starts searching. He begins aft on the starboard side where Meg sleeps. She doesn't have any books, just clothes and a box of condoms. All the clothes are hers. On the port side he finds Kate's clothes and a few books. He doesn't recognize any of the titles except *Rebecca*. He thumbs through *Rebecca* and is surprised to see that Kate has scribbled on many of the pages, though the only marks he can decipher are the exclamation points. On the back flyleaf she wrote a note. *The author should have killed the husband instead of Rebecca.*

He turns to the navigation table. He opens the locker underneath where the sextant is stored. He has looked in here before and he doesn't find anything unusual. He pulls out the drawer until it's up against his stomach but it looks like the drawer comes out farther. He pushes it in a little and gets up from the seat. When he tries to pull the drawer all the way out, it seems to be stuck. He uses a flashlight. There is something wedged in the back. He pushes the drawer in a little, reaches in and pulls out an international vaccination certificate, two them, one for Michael Green and one for Gary Henderson. He continues to search the ketch but he doesn't find anything more belonging to Michael or Gary and he doesn't find the first logbook, the one from San Diego to Bora Bora.

Jamie washes everything by hand, all the towels and sheets, even the women's underwear, and hangs them out to dry from lines rigged between the masts. When Meg and Kate return and climb out of the taxi, he can tell they are both in a foul mood, especially Kate's face is grim. They come aboard without looking at the wash hanging out and go below. Jamie follows them and as they light up cigarettes Meg snaps at him, "Jamie, bring some beer." He brings four bottles, sets them on the saloon table and returns to the galley to listen to them argue.

"We had a deal, Kate. No men."

"We have a deal. Nothing's changed."

"You were flirting with him."

"You're crazy. Why would I flirt with that little fat man?"

"I don't know. But we're through with men, remember? That was the deal."

They go around and around the same point until Jamie realizes that jealousy is at the bottom of it. It seems Mr. Wong paid more attention to Kate than to Meg.

They leave Port Swettenham in a perpetual overcast and power again up the Strait. After lunch Jamie sits in the cockpit with Kate. It's pleasant in the cockpit, sitting under the sailing awning and feeling the breeze as the ketch drives through the flat sea.

"You never told me how you sailed across the Pacific. Did you sail to Hawaii first?"

"No. We sailed down the Mexican coast and then across to Nuka Hiva."

"And then where did you go?"

"We sailed through the Tuamotus and the Society Islands and from there to Samoa and then to Fiji where you joined us."

"Did you stop very often in the Society Islands?"

"We stopped at a number of islands, Moorea, Huahine, and Bora Bora."

"You didn't stop at Tahiti?"

Kate looks sideways at Jamie. "Yes, we stopped there. An overrated place, a port that collects all the riffraff of the South Pacific."

"I was on the schooner *Wind Song* and she sailed to Hawaii and then to Fiji. So I didn't get a chance to see Tahiti. Usually everyone who has been there describes it as paradise."

"Maybe it is, for men who never get past the waterfront with its bars and women."

That night Meg visits him in his bunk. She pulls down his shorts and climbs in and straddles him. There's not much space between the bunk and the overhead and Meg bends over him. He looks for her eyes but it's too dark to see anything. He keeps his voice low. "What happened to Michael and Gary?"

Meg freezes and then she puts her hands on his neck. "Don't ever say that again." She starts choking him, so he begins rotating his hips again until she picks up the rhythm and concentrates on it, releasing her hands from his neck. When she collapses on him, she lies quietly for a moment, letting her sweat run off onto him. Then she rolls off the bunk and stands up. "Where did you hear that?"

"Captain Waters asked about them."

"Captain Waters. That crazy bastard was in Tahiti. Kate is right. We should move faster before more boats catch up with us." She leans over him again and he can smell her cigarette breath. "You are with us now. If people ask you, you don't know anything."

"What don't I know?" There is no answer except the slap of her bare feet on the floorboards as she walks through the galley.

Kate sights the Pulo Rimau Light flashing off the southern end of Penang Island and calls Meg. A wind, a little more than a whisper, has come up from the north, and they heave-to and wait for dawn. In the morning Jamie is in the galley making coffee when the engine starts up again. Both Meg and Kate are in the cockpit and he brings them their coffee. He scans the horizon to starboard and spots the Rimau Wreck Buoy. "There's the buoy at the entrance of the Southern Channel." The women look and nod as if they have already seen it. "We may have a strong current in the channel."

Meg looks at him. "What makes you say that?"

"I consulted the oracle." He stoops below and comes back, holding up a volume of the *Sailing Directions*.

"We'll see."

Selene

Jamie can tell from the buoy that the current is running north, the same direction *Selene* is heading. When the ketch enters the channel Meg and Kate smile as they pick up speed.

"At this rate we'll be at the anchorage before noon."

Jamie points back at the buoy. "The current is building. We may have a tide-race."

"What are you talking about?" As soon as Meg speaks the current surges and the ketch broaches to starboard and lies across the channel. Meg tries to bring the *Selene* up but the current overpowers the engine and drives the ketch toward the reef at the edge of the channel. Meg and Kate start shouting as Jamie jumps to the bow and releases the anchor. The chain rattles out and when the anchor catches, the bow swings into the current and the ketch rides just a few yards from the reef.

Jamie throws the leadline in the greenish water. "Three fathoms. Mud bottom."

Kate comes forward and checks the anchor. She looks at Jamie. "How did you know that?"

Jamie coils the lead line. "Remember when we met in Suva? You asked if I knew how to cook."

"Yes. We were tired of our own cooking."

"You didn't ask if I knew how to sail."

During slack water Meg raises the anchor and Kate heads the ketch up the channel between Penang Island and the Malaysian mainland. When they reach the harbor at George Town they anchor near *Sundowner*. After the port officials leave, Meg and Kate go below and get ready for shore. There are a lot of water taxis in the harbor, small junks with a large sweep aft. Meg wants to use them instead of the dinghy. Jamie looks over at *Sundowner*. The companionway hatch is open and the dinghy is tied astern. The Kepplers are on board. Then Debora climbs in the dinghy and rows over to *Selene*. She is wearing a dark green blouse and white shorts, clothes he hasn't seen before. "Hi. Debbie. Do you want to come aboard?"

"Only for a minute." He takes her painter and helps her over the side. They embrace. "I missed you. Every time my mother cooks lunch I think of you cooking lunch."

Meg and Kate come on deck. Meg glares at Debora and then turns to Jamie. "Did you clean up the galley? We want *Selene* shipshape before you go ashore."

"The galley is clean, Meg."

"And since you are going ashore, you can take the garbage and find somewhere to dump it."

Jamie gets the garbage out of the galley and Debora rows the two of them ashore. "Is that blouse silk? Another present from your father?"

"My father buys me whatever I want. That's what fathers are for."

Jamie climbs out of the dinghy and dumps the garbage in a bin on the pier. "Have you been in town yet?"

"No. I didn't want to go with my parents. I rather be alone on the boat."

"Let's walk to the Fort on the point."

"What Fort? How do you know there's a Fort? You just got here."

"Come this way. It's marked on the chart. Fort Cornwallis."

They walk up Market Street and turn north on Penang Street. Shops and teahouses line the street and people crowd the sidewalks. There are a few cars but the street is mainly filled with bicycles, mopeds and trishaws. And noise. They come out on Light Street and walk along the wall of the Fort. Debora puts her hand on the stone. "Put your hand here. It's warm. We should come here at night and make love."

"It's a little too public."

"Yes. People will see and become jealous and make a scene. Jealousy is such a sin, a deadly sin. We will never be jealous." She brushes the sand from the wall off her hand and puts her arms around his neck. "When are you going to ask my father?"

"Debbie, I just got here today."

"I feel restless when you aren't here. How do you feel? Do you sleep with Meg and Kate? I think Kate is the nicer one."

"They are both nice. Meg is a little bossy but I don't think she's the boss."

"Do you want to sleep with them?" She points to the cannon overhead. "Don't lie or that cannon will strike you dead."

"I don't think it's loaded."

"That's your answer? Let's go back. I think too much salt water has shriveled your brain."

A boat slowly sails up the channel. Jamie looks through the binoculars. *Dodona*. Captain Waters is on the bow preparing the anchor as the tide carries the sloop to the other side of *Selene,* away from *Sundowner*. Jamie waves but Captain Waters doesn't glance in his direction.

Jamie grabs two bottles of beer and hails a water taxi. He points the boatman to *Dodona* and before he leaves the taxi, he hands the boatman one of the bottles. Captain Waters is sitting in the cockpit and Jamie sits down across from him. Captain Waters looks at the bottle in Jamie's hand. "I don't drink that."

"It's not for you. It's for the water taxi. You sailed up the Strait? We didn't have any wind."

"There is always wind. You need to know where to find it." He points to *Selene*. "You found something on the boat."

"I found these." Captain Waters looks at the vaccination cards but doesn't touch them.

"You don't need those. You need retribution."

"I don't think it's my responsibility. It's something for the police"

"You serve a higher authority." He points at *Selene* again. "You sail on that boat and you are intimate with them."

"You know, you sound a little crazy."

"I do not sail with murderers."

When Jamie returns to *Selene*, Meg and Kate are smoking in the saloon. He tries to walk past them to the galley but Meg puts her leg out and stops him. "Where have you been? Running after that little Keppler thing?"

Jamie looks at Meg. "Her name is Debora. I was on *Dodona* talking with Captain Waters. He sailed up from Singapore without an engine. There was plenty of wind. It seems we were unlucky."

"You should stay away from him. He's only trouble."

Jamie moves away from the smoke. "What kind of trouble? He just seems a little eccentric."

"He's a terrible gossip and lies about things he knows nothing about."

"He says he was in Tahiti when you were there. Is that true?"

Kate cuts in, "What's for dinner?"

Jamie looks from Meg to Kate. "We have a lot of eggs. I was thinking of making some omelets."

"We had eggs for breakfast. Make some pancakes and get out a jar of strawberry jam."

Jamie goes in the galley and starts making pancake batter. It's too early for dinner. He lets the batter rest and climbs out the forehatch. The tidal current is running across the wind and he watches as the boats swing on their anchors, back and forth, between the wind and the tide.

Meg shouts from the saloon, "Jamie, brings some beer."

Jamie stands in the cockpit drinking his morning coffee. A tramp steamer enters from the north and drops her anchor below Swettenham Pier. Her awnings are already rigged and the crew are setting up a windsail on the fo'c'sle. Jamie gets out the binoculars. The windsail is a simple canvas cylinder with a square head to catch the wind and a tail end leading belowdecks. Jamie goes in the forepeak and rummages until he finds some light canvas. He takes the canvas and the bosun's bag to the foredeck and begins sewing. Now and then he looks up and watches the water taxis gliding about the harbor. When he is finished sewing he ties the square head of the windsail to the lifelines, sets the tail down the forehatch and he goes aft to the cockpit and watches as cigarette smoke swirls out the companionway.

Meg shouts, "Jamie, what are you doing. Are you going to make lunch or not?"

Jamie climbs down the companionway to the saloon where the two women are smoking. "I thought I would go ashore to the Jade Garden and buy some fried noodles."

"Your job is to cook food, not buy it."

Kate breaks in, "C'mon Meg. I like their fried noodles. So do you."

"Okay, okay. You two can put the dinghy over the side so you don't waste any more money on water taxis."

"Using water taxis was your idea."

"My idea? Which one of us gets ideas around here?"

"Don't start that."

Kate follows Jamie topside. They unlash the dinghy and lower it over the side. Jamie holds the painter. "What ideas were you two talking about?"

Kate smiles. "Meg is good at a lot of things but she doesn't have much imagination. Remember, I'm the one that had the idea to hire you. Now, go get our lunch."

Kate turns and walks aft. "So it was your idea then."

Kate turns back. "What?"

"That you two sail *Selene* together."

Kate loses her smile. "Be careful with what you say. I may get some more ideas."

Jamie waits as Debora rows over to *Selene*. "Are you ready to go?" Jamie nods and climbs in the stern of the dinghy and Debora rows ashore. "My father said you needed to buy canvas for something."

"Yes, he came over to *Selene* and looked at the windsail I made and then asked me to make one for *Sundowner*."

"Does it work?"

"It works fine. It blows cigarette smoke out the companionway hatch, at least as long as the tide isn't running."

Debora, "Well, no one smokes in the cabin on *Sundowner*. After you buy your canvas I have to do some shopping too. Then we can go to a restaurant for tea, just the two of us . . . or do you have to be back to cook?"

"No, Meg and Kate are eating in town tonight."

The street lamps are lit as they come out of the restaurant and Debora takes Jamie's hand and leads him down the street. "Come. I want to show you something." They walk up the street, going farther inland than he has been before. When they turn the corner of the next street she stops. "Look. Isn't it wonderful?"

He looks down a street with two-story colonial buildings on both sides, shops below and apartments above. The second story juts out, forming an arcade over the sidewalk. It's a handsome street, though similar to others, just less crowded. "I don't see it." Then she points and he sees the street sign. *Love Lane*. He smiles. "Yes, it's wonderful."

They walk down the street, hand-in-hand. "Buy me something here."

"I'll have to use your father's money."

"No worries." They look in a shop window. There's a display of bracelet charms. "Buy the elephant."

"You don't prefer the dolphin?"

"No. An elephant has a long memory. Buy the elephant and you will love me forever."

They leave the shop and walk to the end of Love Lane and turn toward the Fort. "You asked my father to join us on *Sundowner*, didn't you?" A sea wind blows down a side street and catches them as they cross to the Fort. "What did he say?" Jamie leads Debora around the other side of the Fort and out of the wind. "What did he say?"

"He said okay. He said I should come over to *Sundowner* and do some work so your mother can get used to me."

"That's a good plan. My mother doesn't take to people right away." She puts her arms around his neck. "I'm sorry I asked you about Meg and Kate. I don't care what happens on *Selene*."

"Why do you bring it up?"

"I don't know. I think they treat you like a girl." She turns to the wall. "Look, this wall is our shelter. It protects and watches over us."

"But anybody can see us here."

"They are just pedestrians. They don't matter. If they come too close the guns on the wall above will shatter them." She pushes him against the wall and starts kissing him.

"Debbie, what are you thinking?"

"She breaks away and looks at him. "What is . . . You have a stiffy, don't you."

"I'm always stiff with you."

She smiles. "On *Sundowner* we'll sail across a blue ocean under a tropical sun and you'll be stiff for days and days on end."

Jamie waits until the tide is almost slack and then he rigs the new windsail on *Sundowner's* foredeck. Keppler joins him and together they watch as the light wind from the northwest fills the canvas.

"I'll go below and see if we are getting any air." Keppler walks aft and Jamie surveys the harbor. Captain Waters is watching him from *Dodona*. Jamie waves but Captain Waters doesn't reply. Keppler returns with a smile. "It's a beauty and the missus is very pleased . . . I'm looking forward to having you on board."

"Do you plan to sail to the Seychelles after India?"

"I don't think so. What's in the Seychelles?"

"You know, there's no airport there. You can only get there by boat, so it must be unspoiled." He points to *Dodona*. "You could talk to Captain Waters. He has been there a number of times."

Keppler looks over. "I've been meaning to talk to him. He must be full of sea stories. Do you want to come with me?"

"No. I want to start working on the bowsprit, get it ready to varnish before I have to return to *Selene*." Jamie picks up a sheet of sandpaper that Keppler has laid out for him but instead of working on the bowsprit he watches Keppler row over to *Dodona* and climb aboard.

Keppler returns to *Sundowner* and walks forward to the foredeck. Jamie climbs off the bowsprit. "What did Captain Waters say?"

"If half of what that crazy pommie suggests is true, you should move over to *Sundowner* as soon as you can."

"He said you should look for Michael and Gary?"

"No, he said you are doing that."

"What did he say about the Seychelles?"

"We didn't talk about them."

Just before midnight a Sumatra squall sweeps into the harbor, bringing gale force winds and monsoon rains. As Jamie lies in his bunk he feels *Selene* lurch into something and then he hears a rasping sound of metal-on-wood. He climbs out the forehatch. The tidal current has driven *Selene's* bowsprit into *Sundowner's* rigging. Meg and Kate appear on deck and then Keppler climbs into his cockpit, runs forward and tries to push *Selene's* bowsprit free. Meg grabs the boathook and starts pushing *Sundowner* away. Debora pokes her head out the forehatch and then as heavy rain sweeps across the deck she disappears again. The boats surge against each other and there's a crushing sound as *Selene's* bow comes down on *Sundowner's* rail. Keppler falls back against *Sundowner's* mast and as he tries to stand, the boats surge apart and he falls again. Keppler gets up and heads aft and Debora climbs on deck, jumps over to *Selene's* bow and dives below. Both Keppler and Kate start their engines and attempt to keep the boats apart but they don't have much control as the tidal current is running across the wind. Jamie finally gets the brake free on the anchor winch and lets out more chain and *Selene* falls aft and swings away from *Sundowner.*

Jamie checks the bowsprit for damage but it's too dark to see clearly. Meg and Kate come forward, Meg cursing the wind and the rain and *Sundowner*. Jamie points to the bowsprit. "We'll be able to see more in the morning." They continue to peer in the dark until more monsoon rain streams across the deck, forcing them below. Jamie goes in the galley and puts water on for coffee as Meg and Kate start stripping off their wet clothes. Water drips off him as he stands in the galley, listening to Meg in the saloon complaining about *Sundowner* dragging her anchor. Jamie goes into the saloon and sets the coffee and cups down on the table. "You anchored too close to *Sundowner*. That and the tide is why the boats fouled each other."

Meg stares at Jamie for a moment, then takes the coffee pot and pours a cup. "What do you know. Go hit the sack. We'll want breakfast first thing in the morning." Jamie goes into the forepeak and undresses in the dark, letting his wet clothes fall to the floor. He climbs in his bunk and finds Debora waiting for him. "Nobody saw me."

Before dawn Jamie climbs out of his bunk and gets dressed. He gives Debora some dry clothes and then they climb on deck. Jamie brings the dinghy up to the bow without bumping it against the ketch and they climb in as quietly as they can. As Jamie rows over to *Sundowner*, Debora puts her feet between Jamie's legs. "You row so beautifully. Row ashore and we can find coffee somewhere and watch the sunrise."

"You aren't serious."

Selene

"Every bit serious." She laughs. "My mother would have such a fit." They reach *Sundowner* and Jamie holds the dinghy steady as Debora climbs out. He hands up her wet clothes and as she takes them she looks down at him with a smile on her face. "Watch for me. I'll come again."

Back on *Selene* Jamie makes coffee, carries the pot and cups to the saloon table and climbs on deck. The sky is clear and the sun is bright in the east. He walks forward and examines the bowsprit. The shackle on the end of the bobstay is damaged and needs to be replaced. Kate joins him and then Meg comes, mumbling about "that bastard Keppler." They agree that the damage is minimal but Meg isn't satisfied.

"Jamie, row us over to *Sundowner*. I wanna talk to Keppler. I wanna know—"

"Let's have breakfast first, Meg. We can go over later."

After breakfast the three of them climb in the dinghy and Jamie rows them over to *Sundowner*. Keppler has his engine running and he is on the foredeck raising his anchor. As soon as they are close enough, Meg begins shouting above the rumble of the diesel engine. "Don't Aussies know anything about anchoring? Your boat dragged her anchor all over the harbor. You almost broke off our bowsprit."

When his anchor is at the stemhead Keppler walks aft to the cockpit. "I think your boat sheered into mine. How badly is your bowsprit damaged?"

"We'll take care of our bowsprit. I just wanna know when you are going to apologize for your poor seamanship."

"You want me to apologize for the Sumatra too?" He puts his engine in gear and slowly heads farther up the harbor, and then he goes forward and drops his anchor and pays out the anchor line.

Meg tells Jamie to row closer to *Sundowner*. "What is this bullshit? Are you trying to avoid me?"

Keppler shuts off his engine and looks at Meg. "Bloody right I'm trying avoid you. I talked to Captain Waters and he gave me an earful."

"What are you talking about?"

"I think you know what I'm talking about. Where are your husbands? Where are Michael and Gary?"

A few nights later Jamie wakes up. Meg and Kate are on deck, moving around. He waits for a few minutes and then looks out the hatch and sees them rowing over to *Dodona*. They climb aboard and disappear down the companionway. Jamie hears oarlocks behind him. Debora rows up and he waves her to the

Selene

bow of *Selene*. "Give me you painter." He ties the dinghy to the bowsprit shroud and helps Debora aboard.

"Were you waiting for me?"

"Of course, Debbie. Quick now. Meg and Kate are rowing about the harbor. Go below before they see you."

"Rowing about the harbor this time of night?"

"Yes, they have someone to visit."

Debora giggles. "I can't picture it. They're too old for that." She climbs below and Jamie stands in the hatch, watching the flashlight as it waves in and out of the portholes in *Dodona's* cabin. "Aren't you coming?"

"In a minute, Debbie." The light goes out on *Dodona* and the outlines of Meg and Kate appear in the cockpit. He tries to see if Captain Waters is with them when Debora yanks down his shorts. He lowers himself into the forepeak and Debora hugs him as he slides into the bunk.

A few days later a launch motors up to *Dodona* and a man in a white tropical suit steps into the cockpit and goes below. When the man climbs back on the launch and it heads for *Selene*, Jamie goes aft to get out the fenders. He catches the launch's bowline and the man in the white suit steps aboard. Meg comes out the companionway, followed by Kate.

"What's this about?"

The man takes off his Panama. "My name is James Loomis. I represent the Chartered Bank of Penang. We are hoping you can help us locate Captain Waters, the owner of *Dodona*."

"We haven't seen him in the last few days."

"Is that so? We understand that you visited his boat a few nights ago."

"Who says so?"

Loomis smiles. "Two white women in a small boat. Half of the water taxis in the harbor saw you. So tell me what happened?"

Kate pushes Meg back. "Yes, we went over to see Captain Waters. We met him in Tahiti and since then he keeps spreading rumors about us wherever he goes. We went over to talk to him, to ask him stop. But he wasn't there."

"He wasn't there. But why would you go talk to him in the middle of the night?"

"He's already spreading rumors about us here and we didn't want anyone on the other boats in the harbor to see us and get the wrong idea."

Loomis looks at the two women in the cockpit dressed in t-shirts and shorts, no shoes and no bras, then looks at Jamie standing at the mainmast, a younger man, blond and tanned. Loomis turns back

Selene

to the women. "I see. Well, if he turns up on his boat please let the bank know." Loomis puts his Panama back on, climbs in the launch and waves the helmsman over to *Sundowner*.

Jamie wakes up in his bunk with Meg slapping him on the head and yelling about whores. He pulls the blanket over Debora, climbs out of the bunk and pushes Meg out of the forepeak and shuts the door. He should put a lock on it. He turns to Debora. "This isn't going to make anyone happy."

Debora throws the blanket off and holds out her arms for Jamie. "Come. It makes me happy."

Meg pounds on the door and yells. "Get that little whore off the boat."

Jamie picks her clothes off the floor and hands them to her. "Get dressed. Maybe you can get back to *Sundowner* before you parents find out."

Debora smiles. "Let them find out. It's about time they grew up." Jamie gets dressed but Debora just lies in the bunk smiling at him. "You pretend like Meg and Kate are your parents."

"They're more than my parents and they're dangerous."

"You're kidding. That's jealousy beating on the door. She wants to take you away from me. My mother told me some older women get like that sometimes."

Kate is in the galley now. "What's going on? Is someone in there with Jamie?"

"It's that little Keppler whore."

"Debbie, please get dressed."

"Kiss me first." He leans over and she grabs him around the neck and pulls him into the bunk. Her body is warm. "Come. We won't be able to do this on *Sundowner*."

A launch flying a large Malaysian ensign heads for *Selene*. Jamie gets the fenders ready. The launch comes alongside and two Malaysian police officers step aboard, an inspector and a sergeant. Meg climbs out of the companionway. "What's this about?"

The inspector is polite but unsmiling. "We request Mrs. Green and Mrs. Henderson to come with us."

Kate follows Meg. "Is this about Captain Waters? We told the man from the bank everything we know."

Inspector looks at the women with mild distaste, "Please dress in something more decent."

"What?"

The sergeant whispers in the inspector's ear. "Yes, something more modest . . . for the Superintendent." The officers wait as Meg and Kate put on blouses and trousers. When they return to the cockpit the inspector circles his head with his hand. "You have scarves perhaps?"

Jamie watches the launch head for the police landing and when he turns to go below, Debora rows up. "Jamie, was that the police?"

"Yes, but I don't know what it's about."

She ties the dinghy to the bowsprit shroud "It's because they call me ugly names."

"Stay there, Debbie. We'll go ashore."

They walk to the Jade Garden and eat a late lunch and then they walk along Victoria Street and over to Beach Street until they come to the Fort. Debora puts her hand on the wall. "I will always remember this place, the sheltering wall. It's a real wall but not a real place. It's a dream place where love flourishes."

"Debbie, your parents aren't going to the Seychelles."

"We are going to India. After that the Red Sea and the Mediterranean. And Europe. Just think, we will see Greece and Italy and—"

"I can't go with you. I have to go to the Seychelles."

She stops and turns away from the wall. "Why? What's so important about the Seychelles?"

"I told you before. The schooner *Stella Maris* is there. I have to bring her back to San Francisco."

"That's crazy, Jamie. You don't even know how to sail. You're just a cook."

He puts his hands on her shoulders and the silk slides over her skin. Is she beginning to cry? "Debbie, a love like ours is a matter of chance. The sea brings us together and then pulls us apart."

"You make it sound like the tide. It goes back and forth, up and down, and in and out."

Jamie looks over her head. "Love is like the tide. That's a good comparison."

"It's not. It's absolutely stupid. Love is too important to leave to chance and the movements of the moon."

"Debbie, look at us. Love happens. It's not something we do. What I have to do is waiting for me in the Seychelles."

"You are going to leave me for a boat?"

"It's not just a boat. It's my inheritance."

Debora pushes herself away from Jamie. "You are serious, a serious fool."

"Debbie, this is no way to say good-bye. You're going to be sailing to a lot places and you'll be saying good-bye to a lot of people. It's part of what we do."

"And I thought you were different, a sweet boy cooking for two bossy women. Now I'm the fool."

Selene

She walks out to Beach Street, waves to a trishaw and sits in the front seat. As the driver pedals away she throws something in the street. Jamie walks to the street and picks it up. The elephant charm. What could he say? They will meet again somewhere? In the Mediterranean? Maybe, but he can't promise that.

As Jamie walks away from the Fort, a tall man in a white-linen suit steps in front of him. He is clean shaven and his gray hair is combed back. "Go aboard. Your boat is getting underway." The man hails a water taxi and speaks to the boatman in Malay before turning back to Jamie. "Go aboard. The boatman will take you."

Jamie stares at the man. A glittering eye in a weather-beaten face. "Captain Waters . . . has something happened?"

"Something is always happening. Go aboard."

"What's happening?"

"The sea is waiting. Go aboard." He turns and walks up a side street and disappears around a corner. The boatman says something and Jamie climbs in.

Meg is on the foredeck of *Selene*, hauling in the anchor. Jamie climbs aboard. The engine is running and Kate is at the helm. "Meg wants to leave you behind. I made her wait." Meg signals to break out the anchor and Kate put the engine in gear and the ketch moves slowly forward. Meg hauls the anchor up and secures it on deck and as the ketch heads past *Sundowner*, Jamie sees Debora at the mainmast. She looks at him with her arms stretched out. Is it good-bye or is she pleading for him to jump in the water and swim to her?

Kate steers the ketch around the northern point of Penang and sets the course for Great Nicobar Island. "Go get dinner, Jamie. They didn't feed us in town and we're hungry."

Jamie prepares dinner and carries Meg's plate into the saloon. Kate comes below. "Let me take that. You stay here and keep out of Meg's way."

"What is she mad about?"

"With you, everything. Just stay away from her."

Jamie makes coffee and then goes in the forepeak, opens the hatch and looks out. There's no wind and the ketch gently rises and falls as she slides through a calm sea. The sun sits on the horizon and when it disappears it quickly turns dark. To port the light on Penang Island flashes. He goes below and lies in his bunk. He could make a cake. Meg would like that.

Later he hears someone on the foredeck. He looks out the hatch and feels a light wind on his neck. Kate, little more than a shadow in the starlight, stands on

Selene

the cabin top. He climbs on deck and Kate walks the boom to the mast, removing the gaskets from the mainsail. "Set the main." She goes aft and slacks the sheet and lifts the boom out of its crutch and Jamie hoists the mainsail. Kate raises the mizzen and Jamie raises the headsails and Meg switches off the engine and the night is hushed.

They are close-hauled on the port tack, making little headway as the sails fill and collapse in the light air. Jamie stands in the bow as water washes against the side of the ketch. Meg and Kate talk and then Kate takes the helm and Meg goes below. Kate's watch. Jamie goes aft and sits in the cockpit with Kate. They don't talk but Jamie senses that Kate likes the company. Near the end of her watch, Kate gives Jamie the helm. She takes the bearing of the Muka Light, reads the taffrail log and goes below to plot their position. When she comes back on deck, Jamie goes forward and stands next to the mainmast. In the west a cloud bank is forming, blanketing the horizon and putting out the stars one by one as it moves toward them.

The wind come up during the night and Jamie wakes as the ketch comes about on the starboard tack. Kate on the foredeck, yells at Meg, "Head into the wind." The jib sheet is caught on something. The ketch heels over and Jamie rolls out of his bunk. He pulls the canvas from beneath the mattress and rigs the bunk-board. While he is climbing back in his bunk a strong wind hits the ketch. Something carries away. The jib sheet. The sail snaps in the wind. The ketch turns and begins running downwind. Jamie climbs out the forehatch and helps Kate lower the mainsail. Kate lowers the jib and Jamie secures it to the bowsprit. Meg lashes the helm and the ketch ride easy, hove-to under staysail and mizzen. He and Kate stand at the weather shrouds, watching the sea build up. "Go below and heat something up." Jamie goes in the galley and looks through the cans of soup. A lot of tomato because they don't like it. He opens a can of chicken noodle and heats it. Kate comes in the galley and takes the cups of soup back to the saloon. Jamie goes in the forepeak and gets out the canvas covers for the forehatch and the galley skylight and then goes on deck and secures them in place. He walks back through the saloon and picks up the empty cups. Meg and Kate ignore him as they strip off their wet clothes and let them drop on the floor. "We'll reef the main in the morning." Meg nods. Jamie cleans up the galley and checks that everything is secure.

Selene

The wind continues to blow through the night and into the next day. There's no cover over the saloon skylight and as the wind blows spray under the dinghy, water drips down on the table and the lee settee. Jamie walks quietly through the saloon, past Meg sleeping in her bunk, and joins Kate in the cockpit. The ketch is close-hauled on the port tack, driving into a heavy sea. He sits next to Kate at the helm and gives himself to the motion of the ketch.

"Tell me, why didn't you join *Sundowner*?"

Jamie hesitates. What does she want to know? "It's a choice I made."

"You don't have to be diplomatic. What did you tell Debora Keppler?"

"I said I signed on *Selene* until the Seychelles."

"That means you got tired of her?"

"No, not that at all. Wait a minute and I'll tell you." He goes below, heats up the coffee and brings two cups back to the cockpit. "My uncle told me to go to the Seychelles and get a schooner. He said I have to bring her back to San Francisco. It's a condition of my inheritance. He said it's in my father's will."

Kate laughs. "I was wondering why you put up with the two of us."

"Why do you say that? You're alright. Even Meg is alright most of the time. You both work together without complaining. That's the main thing on boat."

"Jamie, when did you learn to sail?"

"I don't know. That's like asking when did I learn to walk. My oldest memory is of me and my father in a small boat on San Francisco Bay. The wind comes up and the boat starts taking water. When we turn back, my father keeps saying, 'Bail, Jamie, bail.' I dream of it sometimes." During the night Kate joins Jamie in his bunk and embraces him from behind. He tries to turn to her but she doesn't let him. "Lie still, Jamie. I'm just going to hug you for a minute."

Jamie brings Kate a cup of coffee during her afternoon watch. He looks at the water washing along the lee side. "We aren't making more than two knots."

"Check the log."

As Jamie steps to the stern and bends to read the taffrail log, Meg comes in the cockpit. "What are you two doing? I can't sleep if you're gonna jabber all the time." Jamie straightens up and Meg looks at him. "We should have left you in Penang so you can help Captain Waters spread rumors—"

"I never said anything except to you, Meg."

Selene

"You've probably been telling everything to that little Keppler bitch you've been screwing. Did you think we were gonna stand for that on this boat?"

"I don't see why you should complain about who screws who on this boat."

"You son-of-a-bitch." She suddenly steps toward him and shoves him with both hands, not too hard. The stern of the ketch falls on the back of a wave, forcing Jamie to sit down in the mizzen sheets.

Kate turns around. "Goddammit, Meg. He could have fallen overboard."

Meg laughs. "It's what happens on this boat." She goes below again.

Jamie sticks his head out the companionway hatch. The dawn is overcast and the sea is gray and white. Kate is at the helm and the ketch is beating to windward, straining to make progress in the heavy sea. Spray whips across the deck and catches him in the face. He ducks back below and starts breakfast. The galley is unsteady as the ketch pitches into the sea. He lights the stove and makes coffee. Kate comes in the galley and Jamie hands her the pot and two cups. He sets his cup down and starts frying onions. He adds some potatoes he parboiled the day before and then cracks two eggs in the second frying pan. The sails and rigging rattle and he looks up and listens. The ketch rises and falls in the sea and Jamie braces himself with one hand and stops the gimbled stove from swinging too wildly with the other. He hears seawater slosh through the skylight over the saloon. The ketch settles on the starboard tack and he goes in the saloon and tightens the screws on the skylight. When the food is ready he carries a plate of fried potatoes and eggs aft. Kate comes below. "I'll take that to Meg."

A little later Kate comes in the galley with the empty plate. "Meg complains about having eggs again."

"What do you expect? You ordered twelve dozen of them. I was thinking of boiling half a dozen and making an egg salad for lunch."

"Please don't. Try to find some other way to get back at her. In fact, why don't you just drop it altogether."

"Alright. Pancakes for lunch and spaghetti for dinner. The great satisfiers."

"That's better." She reaches her hand out for her breakfast and he hands a plate of potatoes and eggs.

"Kate, give a warning next time you come about."

Jamie wrings out the rag he uses to clean the galley. The ketch surges as she beats hard to windward and he holds on to the counter for a moment. As he hangs the rag over the sink a freak wind knocks the ketch down. He falls against the counter, gets up and scrambles through the saloon, one foot on the cabin floor, the other on the side of the settee. Meg is slumped in a corner behind the helm. The main boom and lower third of the sail are lying in the sea and water is washing over the lee deck and pouring into the cockpit. He releases the mainsheet, spilling the wind from the sail and the ketch slowly rises up and shivers. Water drains off the deck and he scoots over to Meg. "Meg, are you alright?" No answer. Kate appears in the cockpit and together they carry Meg below.

"Look after her. I'll handle the sails." He climbs back on deck and claws down the mainsail and then lowers the jib before going aft and lashing the helm to windward. The ketch begins to ride easier, under staysail and mizzen, falling off and coming up into the wind again. He sets the main boom in its crutch and furls the mainsail and then unhanks the jib, carries it aft to the cockpit and bags it. He sits in the cockpit to catch his breath. The wind lifts up the crests of the waves and sprays water across the deck and into the cockpit.

He goes below and asks Kate how Meg is. "I don't know yet. She's awake now but she'll have to rest for a day or two. She took a nasty blow to the head."

"We're making a lot of leeway. I think we should set the storm trysail."

"Okay." He heads for the forepeak. "Jamie, put on a safety harness."

He drags the storm trysail up to the mainmast and rigs it with the main halyard and the jib sheet. The trysail is set loose-footed and as he hardens in the sheet the ketch begins to plunge into the waves. She makes little headway but at least the wind and sea aren't driving her so much to leeward. He stands the rest of Meg's watch and when Kate comes on deck, she hands him a cup of coffee.

"Why don't we heave-to and wait for the weather to change?"

Jamie looks at the sky to windward. "We could but I don't think it will change anytime soon. I think there's a storm northwest of us, in the Bay of Bengal, and we're catching the back end of it."

The night sky is overcast and the sails are dull shadows in the darkness. The ketch is beating to windward and as the bow plunges into the waves, seawater washes over the foredeck. Jamie lashes the helm and goes below to make coffee. A light is on in the galley. What is Kate doing up? She should be sleeping. Kate's standing in the galley eating olives out of the jar.

Selene

"Kate, if you are hungry I can make you something. How about some fried rice?"

"Yes. I would like that." She closes the olive jar and heads aft to take the helm. Jamies starts the onions and then the vegetables, adds the cooked rice and sauce. He brings the steaming plate on deck and hands it to Kate. He takes the helm and watches her eat.

"Kate, what happened at the police station in Penang?"

She hands him the plate and takes the helm back. "That was curious. They made us wait around for hours and then they gave us our passports and told us to leave Penang."

"I think that was Captain Waters. Somehow he got you thrown out of Penang." The ketch slams into a wave and falls off before heading up again.

"I wanted to stay in Penang." The trysail luffs and then begins to shiver. Kate turns the wheel the down and the ketch falls off again. "This damn sea. We aren't making any progress." She looks at Jamie. "I'm pregnant and I was planning to have the baby in Penang."

"What? I thought you were just gaining weight."

"That's what Meg thinks. Try not to tell her. She's difficult now as it is."

A Good Crew Is Hard to Find

"Is it intentional? Meg always uses a condom."

"No. Gary insisted it was my fault that we couldn't have a child. He said I was barren. Such a nasty word."

"And now?"

"Yes. I want the child."

Seawater washing over the bow, runs down the deck and out the scuppers. "Is that why you asked why I didn't join *Sundowner?*"

"Don't worry, Jamie. I'm not going to make this hard on you."

The wind blows out of the southwest for three days and on the fourth day it is still blowing. The howling of the wind in the rigging has been constant and Jamie doesn't hear it anymore. In the evening Meg comes on deck for the first time since the knockdown and insists on standing her watch. Jamie gives up the helm and stands at the lee mizzen shrouds. Meg takes the helm, studies the sails and then tells Jamie to harden in the trysail sheet.

"Meg, that will just make the ketch loses speed and make more leeway."

"For chrissakes." She moves over to the sheet winch and lifts the winch handle out of its pocket and lunges toward him. "You think you're in charge now?" She swings and hits Jamie on the shoulder and he falls

Selene

into the mizzen shrouds. The ketch lurches to leeward and Meg loses her balance. She reaches wildly for something to hold, fails, and falls overboard.

Jamie shouts man overboard and grabs the life ring and its danbuoy from behind the helm and throws them after her. The danbuoy has a light at the end of its pole but it doesn't switch on. Jamie releases the trysail sheet and heads the ketch on a beam reach as he counts the seconds. Kate is in the cockpit yelling, "Where is she. Where is she." He points. He doesn't want to break his concentration as he tries to keep Meg's position in his mind's eye. He reaches one hundred, brings the ketch about in the heavy sea and heads back on the reciprocal course. Kate goes below for a flashlight. When Jamie reaches one hundred again he waits a moment and then heads the ketch into the wind. Kate is at the main shrouds searching the waves with a flashlight. The ketch pitches into the sea and begins to lose way and then drift to leeward. Kate yells, "There's the buoy." Jamie coils the end the trysail sheet. Kate's flashlight catches the life ring. Meg isn't there. She has on too much foul-weather gear to catch up to them. As the ketch drifts down on the danbuoy and life ring, he picks them out of the water. Kate yells again, "There she is." Meg waves an arm and he throws the line to her. They pull Meg to the ketch and then together they haul her out of the sea and help her below. Jamie hardens the trysail sheet and heads the ketch back on course. He stands the rest of Meg's watch.

Two days after she fell overboard Meg comes on deck. She moves to the windward side and doesn't look at Jamie at the helm. "Get below."

Jamie moves away from the helm. "Are you alright, Meg?"

"Stay in the galley where you belong." He goes in the galley. It's a mess. Dirty pots and plates are everywhere and water is sloshing back and forth over the floorboards. Standing watch and cooking for Kate at odd hours, he didn't have time to clean up. He goes back into the saloon. Kate's bunk is empty. He looks in Meg's bunk. She's not there either. He goes back through the galley and find Kate wedged in the lee side of his bunk sleeping soundly. He goes back on deck and readies the hand pump.

"What did I tell you?"

"The bilge needs pumping and Kate is sleeping." He pumps slowly, maintaining a rhythm until the pump stops sucking water. It's clogged somewhere. He goes below and lifts up a floorboard in the saloon. There is still water in the bilge. He feels around in the water

Selene

until he finds the pump's intake and pulls a pair of panties off the intake grill. He goes back in the cockpit and starts pumping the bilge again.

"I want something hot. A cup of soup."

"In a minute, Meg. I'm almost done here." He goes below and takes off his foul-weather gear in the saloon and then heats up a can of cream of mushroom soup and brings Meg a cup. He pours himself a cup and after drinking it he starts cleaning up the galley.

They've been wet for days. Below deck everything is wet except Jamie's bunk. Kate sleeps there now. The wind has dropped enough to shake out the reef in the mainsail and set the jib again. It's Kate's watch and Jamie sits in the cockpit with her. "How long is Meg going to be like this?"

"She's been angry with you ever since she found Debora in your bunk."

"Has this something to do with Michael and Gary?"

"No."

"No? Then tell me what happened to them."

"Nothing happened. They left *Selene*. We were in Raiatea and they wanted me and Meg to leave the boat and when we said we wouldn't, they left. There was a hundred-foot schooner anchored in the bay. They joined her when it sailed for the Cook Islands."

"What's the name of the schooner?"

She hesitates. "*Starfish*."

"Why are you lying, Kate? No one names a hundred-foot schooner *Starfish*."

She doesn't say anything for a while. "I didn't think you would believe me."

"Then tell me what happened."

"It was an accident. I wanted to teach Gary . . . No. I wanted to test him. I told Meg to throw my sailing jacket in the sea and yell that I fell overboard. I hid in the forepeak. I wanted Gary to worry about me, to come back and get me, get my jacket. But he didn't. Meg shouted that I wasn't swimming and when Gary ran on deck, he dove in the sea like a fool. Then Michael ran on deck and as he and Meg were trying to release the life ring, he stumbled and fell overboard. That wasn't part of my plan. By the time I came on deck Gary and Michael were far astern. I looked but couldn't see them. Meg panicked. She just stood there screaming. I turned the boat into the wind, started the engine and headed back. The trade winds are strong there and it was slow going against a heavy sea. The sails were shaking wildly and I shouted at Meg to lower them. When we got to where I thought they were, I made wider and wider circles. We didn't find them and then it grew dark."

"You didn't report it."

"No. That was a mistake. I should have as soon as we got to Bora Bora but Meg didn't want to. She wanted to sail on and pretend Michael and Gary went home or something and I went along with it." She pauses. "It was a mistake, all of it. I'm sorry for Gary but I'm also angry. I just wanted to teach him a lesson, to make him pay more attention to me . . . Men don't seem to realize that a woman has a breaking point."

The ketch plunging into the night sea doesn't wake him. It's something else, someone in the galley. Kate is coming to warm herself in his bunk. "Kate?" When she doesn't answer he sits up and looks over the bunkboard. The forepeak is pitch black. Suddenly Meg falls against him and something heavy hits his left arm. He swings his right fist and catches her on the side of the head and she falls. He turns on his bunk light. Meg is sitting on the floor holding her head. His left arm hurts and he has difficulty climbing over the bunkboard. He stands over her. "Are you hurt, Meg?"

"You son-of-a-bitch." She slowly gets up and walks back to the saloon.

A Good Crew Is Hard to Find

Jamie finds a winch handle in his bunk. He leaves it there and goes in the galley and collects all the knives and then he goes aft to the saloon. He ignores Meg who is climbing into her bunk and he takes out the toolbox, and collects the hammer, the heavy wrenches, and screwdrivers. He brings them back and drops them in his bunk. He goes on deck. Kate is at the helm. "What are you doing, Jamie?" He ignores her and goes forward and collects the last winch handle. He puts everything he has collected in a pillow case, takes out the drawer beneath his bunk and hides the pillow case inside and puts the drawer back in. He stands in the forepeak for a moment and then he takes the rigging knife out of the bosun's bag and straps it to his waist. He can't sleep now, so he goes in the head and disassembles the lock on the door and then reassembles it on the inside of the forepeak door. He locks the door, climbs back in his bunk and tries to fall into the rhythm of the bow pitching into the sea.

The next morning the wind continues to blow hard. The sun comes out, letting Kate take a few sun sights and fix their position. Jamie watches her work at the navigation table. When she is finished she looks up. "There must be a strong current running against us. We are making very little progress." The ketch pitches into a wave and seawater flies across the deck and down the companionway. Kate reaches up and slams the hatch closed. She looks at the bruise on Jamie's arm. "What happened last night? Meg has a black eye but she won't tell me anything."

"She attacked me with a winch handle."

Kate walks up to Jamie. "She hates you, Jamie. You saved her life and she can't forgive you for it."

"Yes. I see that. Try to keep her away from me." He turns back to the galley.

"What are you going to do?"

"I'm going to bake a cake. You want pears or peaches?"

Later in the day, as Jamie is in the galley letting the cake cool, he hears the head of the jib rip out and Meg go forward and unhank it and carry it below. A few minutes later the clew of the staysail rips out and Meg and Kate reef the mainsail and heave-to. They have only one sailmaker's palm on board, so Meg and Kate take turns repairing the headsails, working late into the night. The next morning they are still sleeping when Jamie makes coffee. He holds breakfast back for an hour and then he carries the staysail forward, sets it and shakes the reef out of the main. He gets the ketch underway again and adjusts the sheets until she holds her course and then he carries the jib forward and sets it. The beating of the jib sheet on the deck wakes Meg and she pokes her head out the companionway. Jamie similes at her. "Coffee's on the stove."

Meg climbs in the cockpit. "Go get it then."

Kate is getting up as he walks through the saloon and when he returns to the cockpit he has two cups of coffee and the cake. Kate takes the cups and hands one to Meg who starts grumbling. "I don't believe this. We've logged over 600 miles since Penang and it's only 360 to Nicobar and we aren't there yet. We aren't even close."

Jamie smiles at Meg's black eye and then hands up the cake. "Peaches and rum. Leave some for afternoon tea."

In the evening the wind begins to abate and the ketch makes better time. Two days later the sky clears and they sight Great Nicobar Island. As they approach a wide bay with a beach ringed by palm trees, the ketch enters the wind shadow of the island and loses way. After so many days of gray skies, the jungle behind the beach seems an unnatural green. Kate starts the engine and Meg lowers the sails. The water is clear and they can see the sandy bottom. Meg drops the anchor and unties the lashings on the dinghy. Jamie helps her put the dinghy over the side. "Cook a soup.

Selene

I'll be back for it later." Meg and Kate climb in the dinghy and Meg rows them ashore. Jamie gets the binoculars and sweeps the bay from north to south. It looks like they are the first humans to come here.

He goes forward and looks over the bow. He can see the anachor resting on the sand and a school of fish swimming past the anchor chain. He goes below and gets out a facemask, a pair fins, and a spear. The fins remind him of Michael and Gary because they are too big for Meg or Kate. He jumps in the water and swims to the reef at the southern end of the bay. He spears a jack fish and as he swims closer to the reef, the face of coral comes into focus and he sees lobsters in every possible crevice, sitting with their antennas testing the water. He spears another jack fish and catches a lobster and then swims back to the ketch. He cooks a fish soup with onions, potatoes, canned green beans and chunks of fish and lobster.

Meg has been to the ketch. She has taken a sail ashore, the old mainsail and she uses it to make a shelter at the edge of the jungle. She returns to the ketch and enters the galley, pushing Jamie out of her way. She smells the soup and then takes the pot, along with bowls and spoons, and rows ashore again. When she returns the empty dishes she takes some blankets to the dinghy.

"What are you doing, Meg?" She ignores him and rows ashore again. For the next few days Meg moves more supplies from the ketch to the shore, food, clothes, a paraffin lamp, and two mattresses. She tells him to stay out of her way and cook.

Jamie spends his morning drinking coffee in the cockpit and watching the camp on the beach as the women sit at a fire. Later he goes diving off the reef. He catches lobsters and at first he eats lobsters three times a day but after a few days they begin to lose their appeal. The white flesh is too rich. It's not the fat. It's the protein. There's too much of it. After a week he can no longer look at a lobster.

Jamie watches smoke rise from the fire on the beach. Every morning after making a fire Meg walks into the jungle. She has found something. A pool or a spring. When he sees her go inland again he dives in the water and swims ashore. Kate is sitting in the shade of the sail, sewing something. Baby clothes? She looks up. "Kate, what are you and Meg doing?"

"I'm going to have the baby here." She looks off at the sea. "I'm not going back to *Selene*."

"You know this sounds a little crazy. There's nothing here and there's no one to help you."

Selene

"Meg is going to help me. She's all the help I'll need. I can't go back to *Selene*. She is not the boat she used to be."

Jamie wakes in the night. Someone is on deck. Then the sound of oarlocks. He looks out the forehatch. Meg is rowing ashore, the white dinghy visible in the starlight. When he ducks back into the forepeak he smells smoke and goes in the galley, grabs the fire extinguisher and turns on the light in the saloon. A wisp of smoke drifts out of the engine compartment behind the companionway ladder. He removes the ladder and then the compartment cover. Smoke pours out, forcing him back to the galley. He starts coughing and has difficulty keeping his eyes open to aim the extinguisher. Even after the fire is out smoke continues to billow out of the compartment and spread across the saloon. He climbs out the forehatch and walks aft to the cockpit and waits. When the smoke finally clears, he gets a flashlight and checks the engine. The fire burned the cables and hoses and most of the paint. Meg must have used paraffin lamp oil to start the fire but the diesel fuel didn't catch. He goes into the galley and makes coffee, takes a cup up to the cockpit and waits for dawn.

When the sun rises out of the sea and drives the shadows from the bay, Jamie swims ashore and walks up to the camp. Meg and Kate are squatting, trying to get a fire going. Kate looks up. "Meg caught some lobsters yesterday. Do you want to join us for breakfast?"

"I want to talk to Meg." Meg looks up. "What happened to Michael and Gary?"

Meg glances at Kate. "Didn't Kate tell you?"

"I want you to tell me."

Kate puts her hand on Meg's arm. "Don't, Meg."

Meg shakes Kate's hand off. "Just because you got a big belly you think I should take all the blame." She looks at Jamie. "Why not? It doesn't seem to matter anymore, at least not here. It was simple. We killed them. Kate hid in the forepeak and I yelled man overboard and I hit them with a winch handle as they came up the companionway. Gary came up first and I hit him on the head and he fell in the cockpit. When Michael came up he stared at Gary lying there and I hit him. He didn't go down at first and I had to hit him again and again. Then Kate came up and we dragged them to the side of the boat and threw them in the sea."

"It was Kate's idea, wasn't it?"

Meg glances at Kate again. "It was a good plan. We got rid of those bastards." Kate has her face in her hands.

"Look at me, Kate."

Kate takes her face out of her hands. "I didn't want you to hate me."

"I'm leaving now. When the child is born, name it Nicobar and when it's old enough, send it to me in San Francisco." He turns and walks toward the dinghy. This is no way to say good-bye. He turns back. "Kate, I don't hate you. I wish you well. Take good care of the child."

She is standing with her hands supporting her belly. "It wasn't my idea to burn *Selene*."

"I know but you didn't stop Meg either." He pushes the dinghy into the water and rows out to *Selene*.

Jamie hoists the dinghy on board and lashes it over the saloon skylight. The wind is light from the southeast. He raises the main and mizzen and goes forward and hauls in the anchor chain until the anchor is up-and-down. He raises the staysail and breaks out the anchor and while the ketch heads for the northern end of the bay, he hauls the anchor to the surface. He tacks to port and heaves the anchor on board and lashes it on deck. When it looks like the ketch will clear the northern point of the island he tacks again and goes forward and sets the jib. As the ketch rounds the northern point he looks back. Meg and Kate's camp is hidden behind the curve of the bay.

The sky is clear and the wind moderate. Jamie heads the ketch into the St. George Channel between Great Nicobar and Little Nicobar. The water is calm as he beats to windward, tacking back and forth to reach the Indian Ocean. Half way through the channel a sloop emerges from the shadows of Great Nicobar and heads on a course to intercept *Selene*. Jamie gets out the binoculars and studies the boat. *Dodona*. He holds his course and when *Dodona* crosses his bow she heads into the wind and heaves-to. Jamie slacks the main sheet and then goes forward and backs the staysail. He waits as *Dodona* slowly drifts toward him. Captain Waters stands at the backstay, wearing shorts and work shirt, his hair tangled in the wind. His voice booms across the gap between the boats. "They confessed."

Jamie stands in the mizzen shrouds. "Yes. I left them on the island, on Great Nicobar."

"Do not go back. They will thrive there."

"Where are you headed?"

"We will not meet again."

Gloria Fontaine

THE SOUTHEAST TRADE WIND blows across *Selene's* port quarter, driving the ketch toward the heavy clouds sitting on the western horizon. Jamie stands on the stern and casts his fishing line over the side and watches the red-feathered lure until it vanishes in the wake of the ketch. He can't see them, but they are there. Yellowfin tuna. They have been following him for the last seven days. Within minutes a fish strikes his lure and he hauls in his line hand-over-hand. He heaves the tuna up and drops it in the cockpit and with his foot on its head he takes the hook out of its mouth. He cuts out two fillets with his rigging knife and throws the carcass back in the sea. He washes down the deck and the cockpit and after stowing the bucket he looks forward and sees a strip of land sitting under the heavy clouds. Frigate Island.

A Good Crew Is Hard to Find

The next afternoon Jamie watches Mahé Island emerges from a heavy cloud cover. The pilot boat comes out to meet him and leads him through the reef and while passing St. Anne Island, he readies his anchor and lowers the jib and mizzen. The boats in the inner harbor are tied stern-to at the end of the Long Pier and Jamie sails past them, brings the ketch into the wind and drops his anchor. He lets out the anchor chain and the trade wind blows the ketch back toward the pier. There's no one on the pier to take his stern line, so he steps ashore and ties the ketch to a bollard. The steadiness of the land makes him a little dizzy and he steps back on the ketch and furls his sails and clears the lines off the deck.

Jamie waits but no officials come out to *Selene*. The next morning he takes down the quarantine flag, gathers the ship's papers and his passport and walks down the Long Pier. He passes a copra shed at the end of the pier and turns into the main road that runs through the town of Victoria. The road is lined with weather-worn buildings of two stories and corrugated roofs, a few are shops, mostly Indian plus a Chinese-run hotel. Mango trees grow in an open field on the left and on the right, between the buildings, coconut palms lean over the lagoon. Bougainvilleas seem to grow everywhere, climbing up posts and around windows and over fences. Local girls walk past him, wearing bright cotton dresses and narrow-brimmed straw hats. Most are pretty, some are strikingly beautiful.

Jamie walks into the customhouse and presents his papers to an official in a white starched uniform.

"Welcome to the Seychelles, Sir. Do you have anything to declare?"

"Not really, a few bottles of beer and a half-bottle of rum, for cooking."

The official stamps his passport. "Here you are, Sir."

Jamie takes his passport. "I want to ask you something. Is the Seychelles part of the British Commonwealth?"

"No, Sir." He grins broadly. "We are a Crown colony."

Jamie takes a detour up a side road. On the steps outside of a bungalow a girl is sewing a lace collar on her dress. She looks up and waves.

"Bonjour, you come here on a boat?"

"Yes, I arrived yesterday."

She stands up and crosses the yard to the road. She moves with an easy grace that suggests a perfect knowledge of her place in the world.

"You stay here long?"

"I don't know yet. Is it always so overcast here?"

"It is the monsoon. It brings the rain." She stands close to him and he smells coconut.

"You are a beautiful girl."

She frowns. "No, I am not a girl. I am a woman." She walks back to the steps of the bungalow and takes up her sewing again.

As the evening grows dark, Jamie walks out on the pier. Fishing boats are tied next to *Selene*. On the other side of the pier it's too shallow for boats and part of the water is walled off, forming a pool. He walks over and sees the turtles. Not a pool, a pen. He walks back to the fishing boats. A group of young men sitting in the stern of one of boats stops talking and watch Jamie as he approaches.

"Hullo, you come from Bombay?"

"No, from Penang."

"A long way. You come with beer?"

Jamie counts the number of men on the boat. "I think I have a few bottles." The men grin. Jamie steps on *Selene* and puts five bottles of beer in a bucket and steps back on the pier. It's dark now and a light on the pier blinks on. He hands the bucket across to one of the fishermen and another one helps him aboard.

Gloria Fontaine

The bottles are passed out and the men talk again in Creole. Jamie sits on the bulwark with a bottle.

"Do you catch sea turtles?"

The men stop talking and turn to him. One of them moves over to the bulwark next to Jamie. "We catch everything, turtles, tuna, shark, barracuda—"

"Yes, we catch the devil too." They laugh and speak among themselves again.

Jamie smiles. "What do you do with the turtles?"

"We eat them."

"You don't sell their shells?"

"No. They are green turtles. Their shells are of no use . . . You want to ask something."

"Yes. Do you know of a schooner called *Stella Maris?*" The fisherman shakes his head. Jamie takes out a photograph and holds it up. "Here's a picture of her under sail. She must have been here some time last year."

The fisherman holds the photograph to the light and then passes it around and asks the others in Creole. At first no one says anything. Then a man sitting in the shadow of the cabin stands up. "You ask Captain Jack Carter. He comes tomorrow, maybe next day. He sails to the Outer Islands."

The afternoon trade wind blows across the shallow water of the reef and the boats tied to the Long Pier snub on their anchor lines. An eighty-foot trading schooner sails through the reef without a pilot boat. Her main topmast is missing, broken off at the truck. The schooner sails before the boats tied to the pier and the crew drops her anchor just beyond *Selene*. The wind blows her back until Jamie can read her name on the transom. *Marie Louise*, Victoria. There's a large crew of Creoles on board and the captain, a young man, dark but with sandy hair, walks ashore as soon as the gangplank is down. When he sees Jamie watching at him, he grins. "Lost my topmast this time out."

"Are you Captain Jack Carter? Can I ask you something?" He holds up the photograph of *Stella Maris*. "Have you seen this schooner?"

Carter takes the photograph and looks at it. "That's the *Gloria Fontaine*." He hands the photograph back. "She at the plantation in Heron Atoll."

"Do you ever stop there?"

"Now and then. Not very often now that Fontaine has his own schooner." He starts to walk away.

"Wait. Can you tell me where Heron Atoll is?"

He points. "South by southwest, about two days." He looks at Jamie. "Not a nice place to visit."

Gloria Fontaine

In the early morning light Jamie studies his chart of the Indian Ocean. A few scattered specks represent the Seychelles Islands. Heron Atoll isn't one of them. When he takes his coffee up to the cockpit to watch the sunrise, an older man is sitting on the bollard where *Selene's* stern line is tied. Jamie nods to the man and the man stands up.

"I take you to Heron Atoll."

"What? I just sailed across the Indian Ocean. I think I can sail to an island."

"The trade winds do not blow you to Heron Atoll."

"Perhaps not. Can you show me where the atoll is on a chart?"

The man points to the southwest. "It is there, two days in your boat." The man is short with thin gray hair, wearing trousers instead of shorts and a white shirt, wrinkled but clean. He's not Creole.

"Why do you want to go to Heron Atoll?"

"Why do you want to go?"

Jamie laughs. "Okay, come aboard. I can give you a cup of coffee."

The man's name is Arman. "Where are you from?"

"I am from here."

"Were you born here?"

"The people here come from everywhere, from Africa, France, India, Oman, even China. I came from Persia."

"You left out England."

"No, not the English. They do not mix."

"If we sail for Heron Atoll, I can offer you only rice and fish."

"It is enough for me. Even when you don't have the fish."

Jamie stands in the cockpit of *Selene* drinking his morning coffee. The sun is out for a change and he looks at the islands guarding the harbor, two large ones and a number of smaller ones. He tries to remember how the pilot boat led him through the reef. He closes his eyes for a moment. Someone steps on *Selene*. He opens his eyes and sees Arman climbing into the cockpit.

"We leave now. I take the helm. You bring up the anchor."

Jamie is taken aback. "This is my boat. I'll take the helm."

Arman looks at him without smiling. "You know the way through the reef?"

"Okay, you take the helm."

Arman raises the mizzen as Jamie goes forward and raises the mainsail and staysail, letting the sails shiver in the trade wind as he hauls in the anchor. When the anchor is up-and-down, he backs the staysail and the ketch falls off the wind. Arman sheets in the mainsail and heads the ketch toward St. Anne Island. Jamie hauls up the anchor and lashes it on deck and then sets the jib. The ketch picks up speed. They tack between the islands and Jamie handles the sheets.

The ketch clears the pass and Arman heads her toward the southern end of Mahé. Jamie looks at the reefs to leeward. "We are close to the reefs."

"I have sailed this course many times."

"How many?"

"No one has counted them . . . Why do you worry? This is a good boat. She sails well." He points to the top of the mizzen mast and then to the bottom of main mast. "You have a sail for there?"

"A mizzen staysail? Yeah, but I've never set it."

"Set it now."

It's dark as Jamie wakes. Something is wrong. The ketch isn't sailing. He climbs out of his bunk and looks out the companionway hatch. Arman is sleeping on the lee side of the cockpit. Jamie climbs on deck. The ketch is hove-to under mizzen and staysail.

"What happened?"

Arman doesn't move. "It is too dark."

"Why did you heave-to? I can take the helm if you are tired."

"There are a hundred atolls and shoals south of Mahé."

Jamie goes below, makes coffee and brings two cups back to the cockpit. Arman sits up and takes his cup. Jamie sits on the windward side, bracing his feet against wheel pedestal. Dawn is breaking and there is light behind the clouds in the east. "Do you know of a schooner at Heron Atoll?"

"The *Gloria Fontaine*. I am the captain."

"You are the captain of *Gloria Fontaine?* Is that why you are going to Heron Atoll?"

"I take the copra from Heron Atoll to Port Louis." He points forward with his coffee cup. "Look."

A long white line stretches in front of them, waves breaking over shallow water. There are no palms. It's not an atoll, just a shoal.

Arman stands by the helm. "Set the sails" He points between the masts. "The mizzen staysail too."

Gloria Fontaine

Rain whips across the deck of *Selene* as they approaches Heron Atoll from the west. The squall passes and mist rises off the warm land, swirling above the palm trees that cover the atoll. A schooner is moored against a concrete landing on the south side of the pass, her topmasts standing above the palms. Near the landing is a large shed with a corrugated roof and open sides. Jamie lowers the jib and stands ready on the foredeck. The ketch slowly tacks into the pass and Jamie can read the name painted on the transom of the schooner. *Gloria Fontaine*, Port Louis. They slowly sail past the schooner and he looks over her taffrail and along her deck and then up at her masts and rigging. So much bigger. He can't sail her alone. Arman tells him to look to the anchor. Beyond the schooner there is little room to maneuver and the lagoon itself is too shallow even for *Selene*. As soon as they pass the schooner, Arman drops the stern anchor and releases the sheets. The ketch slowly loses way and when her keel scraps the bottom of the pass, Jamie lets go the main anchor. The wind blows the ketch back toward the schooner until she comes to a rest, moored between the two anchors.

Jamie starts clearing the deck, furling the sails and coiling lines. Arman stands in the cockpit watching him. "Put the boat in the water and then put a line there." He points to the bollard at the end of the landing where the bow of the schooner is tied. "And put a line over there." He points to a palm tree on the other side of the pass, beyond the bow of the ketch.

"Aye, aye, Captain."

Arman smile. "Good. Now you understand."

With one quick stroke, Jamie sends the dinghy across the gap between the ketch and the shore, beaching the dinghy next to an island boat resting on the crushed coral beach. The beach is below the landing and he has to walk up a slope to look at the schooner. Arman is at the main shrouds, examing rigging. He turns and climbs down the midship hatch. Jamie studies the schooner. He takes out his photograph of *Stella Maris* but from where he is standing he can't match the schooner to the photograph. He moves farther down the landing next to the mainmast. Lashed to the main shrouds is a life ring with a name painted on it. *Stella Maris.*

Two men approach the landing, coming from beyond the shed, a tall white man in his forties, dressed in white trousers and shirt, and a black man, not as tall but solid, dressed in shorts and a t-shirt and holding a machete in his right hand. The white man waves. "Bonjour Monsieur. I am Aristide Fontaine. This is my plantation." He points to *Selene.* "This is your sailboat?"

"Bonjour M. Fontaine. No, I just use her." Jamie points to the schooner. "This is my boat."

Fontaine raises his eyebrows. "Ah, so this is why you come here. You want to know about the schooner. Captain Arman brought the schooner to me. He doesn't have the means to maintain it, so we become partners. You see, a schooner is very useful here in the Outer Islands. It takes my copra to Port Louis in Mauritius and brings back rice and workers for my plantation. Why do you think this is your schooner?"

Jamie points to the life ring. "Her name is *Stella Maris.*"

Fontaine shrugs. "Many things are found in the sea."

"I have her papers." He takes the papers from his pocket and holds them up. "The bill of sale and a copy of the ship registration."

"Let me see."

Jamie studies him for a moment and then hands him the papers. Fontaine takes out a pair of glasses from his shirt pocket and unfolds the papers. He reads each document carefully. "So you are Jamie Blair." He folds the papers again and puts them in his shirt pocket along with his glasses. "Papers do not mean so much here in the Outer Islands." Jamie starts to speak and Fontaine holds up his hand. "Wait, M. Blair. You see, I too have papers. I have bills that show there was much work to do on the schooner. This is my investment. This means it is my schooner too. If you want to take the schooner away from here, you have to pay me for my investment. You understand?"

"I can give you *Selene*."

"You have papers for it, too?"

"No, she is not mine."

"It is not yours. How do you give it to me?" He looks at *Selene*. "It is a good boat, but too big for here at the atoll and too small to carry copra to Port Louis." He turns back to Jamie. "I prefer to have cash for my investment."

"I don't have any cash."

"I see." Fontaine turns to the man next to him. "Hector, is there some use for M. Blair?"

"We need a boatman."

"Yes, of course. M. Blair, you will work for me. Hector will tell you what you do."

Jamie watches as Fontaine climbs aboard the schooner and then goes down the midship hatch. He turns to Hector. "M. Fontaine didn't say how much he is going to pay me."

Gloria Fontaine

"This is M. Fontaine's plantation. You do what he wants. Come, I show you." Hector walks down the slope to the coral beach and stands next to the fishing boat. He taps the gunwale of the boat with the blade of his machete. "You will take this boat to the camps." He points to the north with the machete. "There are two camps, four miles and eight miles." He points to the sail lying on the thwart of the boat. "The sail is ripped. You row the boat to the camps."

"What happened to your boatman?"

"He is at the hospital."

The boat needs paint but it looks solid. There is a pair of oars, a tiller, and some rain water in the bottom. Jamie climbs aboard and picks up the sail lying on the thwart. It's furled around a yard. He looks up at the short mast and then back at the yard. It's a lugsail. He unfurls the sail and holds it up. It's nothing but shreds. He will have to make a new one. As he climbs out of the boat he sees a girl standing on the landing watching him. She is tall and slim, with long dark hair. When she sees him looking at her, she smiles and walks away. Not a girl, a young woman.

The sky is clear and the midmorning sun is harsh as Jamie watches the bow of the schooner swing out into the pass. Two men on the foredeck set the jib and the schooner slowly heads out to sea. Once the schooner clears of the pass, the crew set all the working sails. She matches the photograph of *Stella Maris*.

Jamie carries the drifter and the bosun's bag off the ketch and spreads the drifter out on the landing. He looks at the station. Trays of copra lie drying in the sun. Close by two men husk coconuts in the shed. Next to the shed is a storehouse and beyond the storehouse is another building, a single-story plantation house with a wide veranda and farther back among the palms are huts where the workers live. Jamie goes back down the slope to the island boat and picks up the lugsail and then arranges its tattered pieces over the drifter, matching the head of the lugsail to the head of the drifter. The drifter is a large headsail used in light winds. He has never used it. He cuts off the upper part to make a new lugsail. He sews the foot of the lugsail, folding over the canvass and using a sailmakers stitch. He looks up now and then to watch the men working in the shed. He sews extra pieces of canvass on the lower corners to reinforce them and then sews cringles for the sail's tack and clew. While he is attaching the head of the new lugsail to its yard, he hears someone approaching. It's the young woman again. The girls of Seychelles wear hand-made dresses of bright cottons from Indian, but the young woman watching him is wearing a dark blue linen dress with wide pleats. It's doesn't look hand-made.

She smiles. "Bonjour Monsieur."

"Bonjour, ah, Mademoiselle."

"People do not often come here."

Jamie stands and furls the lugsail arounds its yard. "No, there doesn't seem to be much to attract people here except work."

She points to the lagoon. "Look. The herons have come."

Jamie turns. Herons are wadding far out on the reef flats. "There's hundreds of them."

"It is a siege."

"A siege?"

"Yes, a siege of herons." She smiles and walks back past the copra shed and into the palms beyond.

Jamie is in *Selene's* galley making coffee when Hector calls him. He climbs on deck and sees that the men have pushed the island boat into the water and are loading it with heavy bags and large demijohns. Hector points to the boat. "Show me the sail." Jamie climbs in the dinghy and pushes himself ashore and unfurls the lugsail, letting the sheet whip in the wind. "Good. You go now. You take rice and bacca to the camps. Remember, four miles by water and then another four miles." Jamie goes back to the ketch and gets a jug of water, his fishing gear, and his hat. When he returns to the shore Hector is still waiting. "You bring back copra from the camps. If the boat is not full, you tell the workers I come next time."

"I go alone?"

"What do you think? We have workers for playing on the lagoon? Go now and maybe you come back before night."

Jamie climbs in the boat and Hector shoves it out into the pass. He ships the oars and rows up the pass and around the end of the northern island. When he reaches the lagoon, he unships the oars and sets up the tiller and then unfurls and raises the lugsail until its yard doubles the height of the mast. He holds the sheet in one hand and the tiller in the other and the boat heads slowly up the lagoon. The shore is covered with mangroves where the herons have their nests. Farther inland he can see the tops of palm trees. After about two miles the mangroves give way to a beach and among the palm trees he sees a hut. It's too soon for the first camp and he sails on.

The water is clear and when he sees fish he gets out his fishing line. He hooks a fish and lets go of the sheet and the tiller and pulls it up to the boat. A three-foot reef shark. He doesn't want the shark in the boat, so he drags it behind. It takes him over three hours to reach the first camp. The copra shed comes into view and four men walk to the beach. They talk loudly in Creole as he approaches. Jamie beaches the boat and steps ashore. The men stare at him until he points to the boat and then they begin unloading the bags of rice and the demijohns of bacca. Jamie shows them the shark behind the boat and one of the men grabs its tail and drags it ashore and with his foot on the shark's head, takes the hook out of its mouth, and then he starts butchering it with a machete.

Trays of copra lie out to dry between an open shed and a pandanus hut. On the other side of the hut is a well-tended garden, aubergines, chilies, cucumbers, tomatoes, a vegetable with large leaves and another plant that looks like potatoes or maybe yams. In front of the hut is an open fire where the men are already drinking bacca and cooking rice and grilling shark steaks. Jamie points to the boat. "Copra." The men look up. One of them stands and speaks in Creole and then he points to the fire. "You eat. You go to other camp and then come here and get copra. Copra ready then."

Jamie eats grilled shark and rice with chiles and other vegetables. The men sit around the dying fire, talking and drinking. They offer him a cup of bacca. It's sweet and mildly alcoholic, made from crushed sugar cane. When he gets ready to leave, they tell him to catch another fish, a grouper or a snapper. He pushes the boat in the water and rows out to the coral heads and lets the boat drift while he lowers the fishing line. The sun breaks through the overcast for a few minutes before clouds rush to cover it again. The herons are out on the reef flats and beyond them he can see a white line where the waves break on the eastern side of the atoll. There doesn't seem to be any land on that side. He hooks a fish, a big one, and holds it up. Some type of parrot fish with a large bump on its head. He rows back to the camp and gives the fish to the men.

It's late and Jamie spends the night at the camp. Hector told him not to let the men steal supplies from the boat, so when the herons fly to their nests, he rows the boat out on the lagoon and anchors for the night. It quickly grows dark and with the overcast there is nothing to see but the embers of the dying fire on the beach. He tries to sleep on the sacks of rice as the talking and laughing from the camp goes on deep into the night.

A light rain wakes him before dawn. He covers the rice with a tarp, drinks some water and waits until there is enough light to set sail. The camp is quiet as he weighs anchor. There is just enough wind to fill the lugsail and the boat barely make a ripple on the lagoon as it heads north along the shore of the island. When the sun rises the herons fly from their nests to search for food on the reef flats to the east.

It's close to noon when he sights the second camp. He beaches the boat and the men come out from the shed. The day is still too wet to dry copra. The men unload the boat and one of the men holds up Jamie's fishing line. The men talk among themselves in Cerole and then one of the men, younger than the others, walks over to Jamie. "The men want you to catch a fish for their dinner."

"Is catching fish the boatman's job?"

"It is the job of the man with a boat and a fishing line. Catch a big fish and make them happy."

"You are not Creole. What are you doing here?"

"What is anyone doing here? What are you doing here?"

"There's a schooner here. She belongs to me."

"The *Gloria Fontaine?* She belongs to Captain Arman. It is an unlucky boat."

"What do you mean? Did you sail on her?"

"Go catch a fish. The men are waiting." He turns and walks away.

Jamie rows the boat out to the reef and lets out the fishing line. When the wind blows the boat back toward the shore, he sets the anchor. He hooks a big silver fish that he doesn't recognize and rows back to the camp. The men seem pleased with the fish and after they grill some steaks they offer him food, fish with rice and vegetables. After eating he looks for the young man who mentioned the schooner. He walks around the camp and then under the palms until he comes to the ocean on the lee side of the island. The reef is only a few yards wide and the ocean laps at its edge. Jamie spends the night at the camp because the men refuse to load the copra in the boat until the next morning. He takes the tarp from the boat and sleeps on the beach.

The sky is clear in the morning and the men set out the copra trays in the sun and then they load bags of copra in the boat. Jamie declines a cup of bacca and rows the boat away from the beach and sets the lugsail. The wind is stronger and the boat makes good time and reaches the first camp by midmorning. The men have the bags of copra ready on the beach and load the boat as soon as Jamie arrives. When the boat is fully loaded the gunwales are only a few inches above the water. The wind is good but Jamie has to sail on a close reach and spray whips over the bow. When it gusts, he lets go of the sheet to keep from shipping too much water. About a mile from the pass the halyard breaks and the yard and sail come crashing down. He tries to fix the halyard but the jute rope is rotten from too much rain and sun. He ships the oars and rows and it's evening when he reaches the pass and beaches the boat next to his dinghy. He walks up to the landing and looks about. No one is there. Off among the palms there is single light at the plantation house.

Jamie breaks out the half-inch hemp rope in the forepeak and carries a coil of it and the bosun's bag ashore. The sun is rising above heavy clouds in the east and the heron flying out to the flates. The men unload the bags of copra from the boat and when the boat is empty, Jamie unsteps the mast. The halyard runs through a hole in the top of the mast and then to the yard of the lugsail. He whips both ends of the rope with yarn, ties one end to the yard and steps the mast again. He raises the sail, letting it dry in the light wind. The young woman in the dark blue dress appears on the landing.

"Bonjour Mademoiselle."
"Bonjour Monsieur."

He walks up to the landing and stands next to her. They both look at the herons on the reef flats. "I've seen where the herons nest in colonies."

"Those are heronries."

He looks at her. "You seem to like the herons."

"They are monogamous."

"My name is Jamie." He waits for her to say her name.

"I know your name. I read the papers you gave my father."

"Then you are Gloria Fontaine."

"That is my aunt's name."

One of the workers shouts something and the woman hurries across the landing to the ocean side. A schooner is approaching the pass. She heaves-to and the crew puts a boat over the side and two men row while a third sits in the stern and steers. Jamie recognizes the man in the stern. Captain Jack Carter. Fontaine arrives at the landing and shouts in French at the boat and waves it away and the men row the boat back to the schooner. The young woman looks at Fontaine and walks back through the palms to the plantation house. Hector comes up to Jamie.

"Why doesn't M. Fontaine let the boat land?"

"You do not to talk to Mlle. Fontaine."

"What? Why not?"
"You do black mans work."

The sun is bright as Jamie stands on the shore next to the island boat. Heat shimmers on the reef flats, making the herons seem to float above the water. On the ocean side of the atoll, squalls rush away to the west. He unships the boat's mast and then walks to the copra shed. Two men are husking coconuts. They strip the husks from the nuts with their machetes, slice the nuts in half and then lay the halves in the sun to dry. Jamie calls them to him with his hand and leads them to the boat. He wants them to help him turn the boat over. The workers are older men with gray hair but they are still strong and they quickly turn the boat over before Jamie can help. He points to himself. "Jamie." Then he points to the two workers.

The smaller worker points to himself. "Louis." And then to the other worker. "Bourbon."

Jamie hands Louis a pack of Meg's cigarettes. They are probably stale but the men are pleased and talk in Cerole as they walk back to the copra shed.

Jamie scrapes the old paint off the bottom of the boat and lets it dry in the sun. Later he checks the seams and patches a few of them with white-lead paste. While he is applying undercoat to the boat,

Hector arrives and watches him. "What do you do?"

Jamie looks up. "I'm working on M. Fontaine's boat."

"You work when you do not need to."

"Does M. Fontaine pay me for not working?"

Hector laughs. "I think you take my job soon."

"How? I don't speak Creole."

"Maybe someone teach you."

The *Gloria Fontaine* approaches the pass under main and staysail. She begins losing way before reaching the landing and a man in the schooner's boat takes a mooring line ashore and the crew warps the schooner up to the landing. The crew and the two copra workers at the station unload the schooner, mainly bags of rice and boxes of Fontaine's personal supplies. The schooner has brought three new men to the plantation and Arman leads one over to the edge of the landing where Jamie is standing. "This man is Jean-Paul. Tomorrow, when you go to the camps, you take him with you, teach him to be a boatman."

In the morning, when Jamie takes his coffee up to the cockpit, the boat is in the water and Hector is supervising the men loading rice and bacca for the camps. Jamie gulps his coffee, throws the dregs over the side and hurries ashore. Arman brings Jean-Paul down to the beach. "You teach him everything. Make him a good boatman."

Jamie and Jean-Paul climb in the island boat and Hector pushes the boat out into the pass. Jamie turns to Jean-Paul. "You know how to row?"

Jean-Paul nods. "How to row."

"Okay, row us up the pass and out on the lagoon." Jamie helps Jean-Paul ship the oars and then he watches as Jean-Paul moves the oars up and down, splashing the water with the blades. Jamie looks back at the landing and sees Arman standing there with a smile. Jamie points to the stern. "Sit there, Jean-Paul."

Jean-Paul moves to the stern thwart. "Sit there."

Jamie rows the boat out on the lagoon, unships the oars, and calls Jean-Paul to the mast. "This is the halyard. It raises the sail. Like this." Jamie raises the sail part way and then lowers it. "Now you do it."

Jean-Paul takes the halyard, raises the sail part way and then lowers it again. "Like this."

Jamie looks at him. "How much English do you speak?"

"Much English."

"Okay, Jean-Paul, you just sit here by the mast." Jamie raises the lugsail, ships the tiller, and heads the boat north. As they sail along the shore, Jean-

Paul points at things, the mangroves, the herons, the clouds, naming them in Creole.

After a while Jean-Paul points to the fishing line in the stern. "You want to fish?" Jean-Paul nods and Jamie hands him the fishing line with the feathered lure. Jean-Paul lets the line out and almost immediately he hooks a fish. He hauls it in, grabs it with both hands and beats its head on the gunwale. It's a blacktail snapper. "Catch another one, Jean-Paul, and we'll have enough for dinner." Jean-Paul lets the line out again and watches the water. Within minutes he catches another snapper.

When they reach the first camp, Jean-Paul jumps out of the boat and starts shouting. The men approach him and he talks rapidly. He hands the fish to one man and he sends another man to the garden. Jean-Paul goes to the fire and looks in the pot. He sniffs and then he takes the pot to the edge of the camp and throws the contents in the bush. The men bring him vegetables, sweet potatoes, tomatoes, chilies and some large leaves. Jean-Paul cuts them up and throws them in the pot and lets them simmer. He adds water and after the pot has been boiling for a while, he adds pieces of fish. When the fish soup is ready, the men stop drinking bacca and gather around the pot. They eat quickly, until the pot is empty. After they have all eaten, Jamie looks at the sun. There's still time to reach the second camp. He calls Jean-Paul but the men won't let him leave.

Jamie sails to the second camp alone. He drags the fishline behind and reaches the second camp in the late afternoon without catching anything. The men come to the beach and unload the boat and then one of the men holds up the fishing line. Jamie pushes the boat off the beach and rows out on the lagoon. He fishes among the coral heads until the sun sets, turning the western half of the sky red. He catches a large grouper and returns to the camp. In the evening, as the men drink bacca, Jamie sits next to the young man he talked to last time he was at the camp.

"My name is Jamie. What's your name?"
"Darian."
"Are you from here?"
"I am from Mahé . . . You want to ask me something."
"Yes, but I thought we could just talk a little first."
"Talk about what?"
Jamie thinks for a moment. "I'm from the other side of the world, but we are about the same age. There must be some things we can talk about."
"Here there is copra and work. You want to talk about these things?"

"No. I want to talk about why you are here."

"I do not what to talk about this."

"Did you sail on the schooner when she was called *Stella Maris?*"

Darian looks at him carefully. "I know what you want. I do not want to talk about it." He stands up and walks away.

Jamie calls after him. "Does Arman keep you here?"

Darian turns back. "If I tell you and Arman finds out, he will kill you."

"Why doesn't he kill you?"

"I am his son."

The sun comes out as the boat nears the station. When the pass comes into view, Jamie sets Jean-Paul in the stern and gives him the tiller and the sheet. He looks at the approach to the coral beach and adjusts Jean-Paul's hands. "Do not move, Jean-Paul."

"Not move."

Jamie sits by the mast with a line looped over the sheet and his hand below the gunwale. He looks up and sees Arman watching from the landing. Just before the boat passes the bow of *Selene,* Jamie jerks the sheet out of Jean-Paul's hand, spilling the wind from the sail and the boat comes to a gentle rest on the beach.

Arman walks down from the landing. "You make Jean-Paul a good boatman?"

Jean-Paul climbs out of the boat. "Good boatman." Jamie walks past the copra shed and under the palms until he comes to the plantation house. It's not a big house, four rooms with a passageway down the middle. From the steps of the veranda he can see through the house to the outside kitchen at the back. It's quiet except for the workers husking nuts.

Jamie calls out, "Bonjour M. Fontaine."

The trade wind shakes the palm heads, and then a chair scraps on a wooden floor and Fontaine appears at the door. "Bonjour M. Blair. Hector tells me you are a good worker."

"That's what I want to talk about."

"You do not like the work?" He is smiling.

"The work is fine. I can maintain the boat as well as supply the camps. I want to talk about my pay."

"I pay you like all the workers on my plantation, in bacca."

"I don't drink bacca."

"I sympathize with you. I do not drink it myself. I prefer Mauritius rum."

"So how much is my bacca worth?"

"Bacca is for drinking. If you do not drink it, perhaps someone else drinks it. But I see what you want. You want cash to pay for the schooner. There is no cash here on the plantation, but the Japanese fishboats have cash. They pay in American dollars for hawksbill shells."

"Hawksbill? That's a sea turtle. Where do I find them?"

"M. Blair, if I knew that I would not need you to look for them."

The sun is rising into the clouds on the horizon. Overhead the morning sky is clear. The workers carry bags of copra from the shed to the schooner and then down the midship hatch. Fontaine stands on the landing next to the schooner talking to Hector. Arman paces the deck of the schooner, watching the crew prepare her for getting underway. When Fontaine steps on the schooner, Arman starts shouting in Creole and the bow of the schooner swings out into the pass. Jamie walks over to Hector and together they watch the schooner sail out the pass under her headsails. Jamie turns to Hector. "Where can I find turtles."

"What kind of turtles you want?"

"M. Fontaine wants me to catch hawksbills. Is it still legal to catch them out here?"

Gloria Fontaine

"They find you with turtles, they take your boat and put you in prison."

"But they have to find me, right?"

Hector smiles and then waves his arm to the northwest. "There are reefs out there where they feed. You look for them there."

Jamie walks over to the bollard and unties *Selene's* stern line and then he rows across the pass and unties her bow line. He climbs aboard the ketch, unrigs the awning and then hoists the dinghy on board. The wind blows across the lagoon and out the pass. Jamie checks the horizon. No squalls are approaching from the east. He removes the gaskets from the sails and goes below to make coffee before setting sail. When the water boils he pours it into the coffee pot.

"A cup for me too."

He turns and sees the young Fontaine woman standing in the doorway to the forepeak. She looks younger in white a blouse and shorts and no sandals.

"What are you doing here?"

"I show you where there are turtles."

"What's your father going to say? He's going to be angry."

"He is already angry. He can't find someone to marry me. In Port Louis they think he is *petit blanc* and they think I am *petit coco*. Now he goes to look for someone in Mahé."

"How do you know where to find turtles?"

"I brought a net to catch them." She points to the forepeak. "It is in there." She turns back to him. "Do you want to catch them with your hands, sneak up on them in the water? Do you think catching turtles is that easy?"

Jamie takes down two cups from hooks above the sink and carries them and the coffee pot into the saloon. They sit across from each other at the table as the sun shines through the skylight and glances off the varnished mahogany. Her brown eyes catch some of the sunlight. She's smiling. She finds this amusing? He pours the coffee. "Will you tell me your name?"

"I am Melia."

"Is that a local name?"

"No, it is not a name from here. It is my own name."

Jamie takes a sip of coffee and then puts his cup down. "I'm afraid I can't take you with me."

"You have so little courage?"

"I can't take you. They will say I kidnapped you."

"You sail alone on a boat and worry about what people will say?" He shakes his head. "No? Do you know what it is like to live here? I have only the herons and they will fly away someday. I do nothing but wait to be married to a *grand blanc* in Mahé"

"What about Hector? He won't let you leave."

"Hector does what I say."

Jamie looks out the companionway at the patch of blue sky. "Maybe we can be back here before the schooner returns."

She smiles. "You are the cautious man."

Jamie stands on *Selene's* foredeck looking at the clear horizon to the west and feeling the afternoon trade wind on the back of his neck. In the pass a weak tidal current carries debris out to sea. He lets out the anchor chain and goes aft where Melia is standing in the cockpit watching him. He hauls in the stern anchor and stows it in the locker under the cockpit. "Can you steer the boat?"

She smiles at him. "I am from the islands. Why do you ask such a thing?"

He goes back to the foredeck and hauls the anchor up short and then sets the staysail and backs it. When the bow of the ketch fails to fall off into the pass, he hauls the anchor up to the surface. The bow turns and Jamie lets out the sheet as Melia steers the ketch past the landing, keeping her in deep water. Jamie sets the jib and hauls in the sheet and the ketch heads out to the sea. He looks aft at the landing. No one is watching them leave.

"There is a reef about twenty sea miles in that direction." She points to the northwest. "The turtles sometimes feed there."

"How do you know that?"

"How do you know anything? I have been there."

She likes to steer the ketch so Jamie lets out a fishing line and soon he hooks a yellowtail. He cuts the fish into steaks and goes below to cook lunch of fried fish and steamed rice.

In the late afternoon Melia sights the reef, a line of broken water in the open sea. "We go to the other side of the reef. See where the waves break in two? We anchor behind the close one."

Jamie puts the anchor over the side, letting it hang from the bow. Melia brings the ketch into the wind and as the boat loses way, Jamie releases the anchor. The wind continues to blow out of the southeast but the water is calm in the lee of the reef. As he lets out the anchor chain he can see the bottom drop off and the water turn dark blue. He goes to the cockpit and takes out a facemask and fins from the locker. Melia watches him. "What are you doing?"

"I'm going to check on the anchor." He takes his shirt off and jumps in the water and follows the chain down to the bottom. The anchor is dug in behind a coral head. He swims back to the ketch and climbs aboard.

Melia points to the dinghy. "Put the boat in the water and then get the net." The net is flaked down in a galvanized tub and he hauls it up on deck. "We put the net between where the two waves break on the reef." Jamie ties one end of the net to the stempost of the ketch and lowers the tub in the dinghy and then he goes aft for the stern anchor and lowers it in the dinghy too.

"You don't have to come. I can do this myself."

"What do you think? You can row the boat and work the net at the same time? You row and I work the net." She climbs in the dinghy. It's an old handmade fishing net and as Melia lets it out, she uses both hands to shake out the tangles. When the net is all the way out, Jamie drops *Selene's* stern anchor, pulls the net tight and ties it to the anchor line. They both sit in the dinghy for a moment and look at the net. It stretches across the gap in the reef where waves break on each side. "The current will drive the turtles in the opening between the waves and the net will catch them."

In the late afternoon she watches him marinate tuna in lime and onions and serve it over pasta. She doesn't cook herself. "We always have a cook. It is expected of us." After dinner they sit in the cockpit and watch the sun turn the western horizon red. He looks at her. So friendly, yet so distant. She smiles at him. She always smiles at him. "You look at me. What do you think?"

"What do the turtles eats."

"That is what you think when you look at me? You think it is time for a school lesson?" She laughs. "The hawksbills eat sponges that grow on the reef but they eat other things too. That is why we do not like the meat. Some of the things they eat have poison, like the jellyfish."

"Have you caught turtles here before?"

"No. It is poaching. We do not use the shells. The Japanese use them to make combs for their weddings. It is a custom they have."

Just before dark Melia scans the gap in the reef. "Look. Something is in the net." They climb in the dinghy and Jamie rows out to the middle of the gap. They are losing the light and when they look in the water the turtle is only a shadow, pulling the net down as it tries to dive. Jamie takes the boot hook and pulls the net up to the dinghy and together they haul the turtle on board, each grabbing a front flipper and dragging the turtle on its back over the gunwale. "It is not fully grown, maybe fifty kilos." Melia examines the turtle. "This one is female. Come. We throw her back." They lift it up again and drop it clear of the net and it disappears in the dark water.

That night as the wind gently rocks the boat, Jamie sleeps in the saloon and Melia in the forepeak. In the morning when he begins to make coffee, Melia comes in the galley. "Check the net first. It is better the turtles are not too tired." The day is overcast as they climb in the dinghy and Jamie rows to the middle of the net. There are two turtles in the net, floating listlessly in the water. Together they pull the net up and haul the turtles into the dinghy. "This one is a green turtle. The shell is no good. We throw it back." They drop it over the side and Jamie watches it swim down into the deep blue water. He checks the anchor-end of the net and then rows back to the ketch.

Jamie climbs aboard and hands down the main halyard to Melia and she ties a sling around a front flipper of the hawksbill and guides the turtle as Jamie hoists it on board. The turtle lies on its back, gasping for air. It's exhausted from struggling in the net. He ties the sling to the handrail on the cabin top. "Do not leave him in the sun. It hurts him."

"Okay. I'll put up the awning."

Later they sit in the cockpit drinking their morning coffee. "The net is a success but one turtle won't be enough."

"It will be enough to show my father you can catch them."

"Won't he know that you helped me?"

She smiles. "He is a man. He does not think a woman can do anything." She looks to windward, studying the horizon. "With the weather like this, we stay here a week." It sounds like a promise.

In the afternoon Jamie throws a bucket of water on the turtle lying near the mainmast. As he is putting the bucket away, Melia comes on deck wearing a red bikini. It's the first bikini he has seen and he stares and when she sees him staring, she smiles, climbs over the lifeline and dives into the sea. He watches her swim in the blue-green water, her dark hair flowing behind her. When she is ready to come out, he puts the boarding ladder over the side and watches her climb up the ladder before he hurries below for a towel. He holds the towel out for her but before she uses it, she takes off her bikini, letting if fall at her feet, and then she dries herself off. She smiles at him, takes his hand and leads him below, leaving the towel and a small pile red cloth on the deck.

In the morning the sun is bright and the clouds are far away on the horizon. After they check the net, Jamie cooks breakfast and then they drink coffee in the cockpit. Later Melia goes about the ketch in her bikini, until she goes swimming, then she takes it off to dry and goes about with nothing. Jamie stares at her. "You are brown everywhere."

"Yes, I am coco. Is that why you stare?" She smiles at him.

"I stare at you because you are the center of all this." He waves his arm. "The sun, the sea, and the wind. The world here admires you. You bring out its beauty."

She looks at him, her head to one side. "How can you sail a boat across the ocean when you have such things in your head? The sun is harsh and the wind is cruel and the sea is a cold grave. Where is the beauty in that?"

"The beauty is here, in what we have together."

She laughs. "Yes, the reef is beautiful but it is not the real world. It is a play world." She takes his hand. "Come, we play while there is still time." She leads him below and they do not return to the cockpit until evening, when they check the net.

They check the net twice each day, mornings and evenings, and at the end of the week they have six turtles tied on deck. When clouds cover the sky and a squall whips rain across the deck of the ketch, they take in the net and set sail for Heron Atoll. They have to beat back against the trade wind and Melia spends long hours at the helm. When Jamie tells her it's time to tack, she tells him to go below, to cook something or to bring her something. She wants to tack the ketch by herself. She wants to be alone on deck.

It takes them two days to reach the atoll. Melia steers the ketch into the pass and Jamie goes forward to the bow and they moor the ketch in the same place as before, between the two anchors. The *Gloria Fontaine* isn't back from Mahé yet and the plantation is still. Hector brings the workers down to the beach and they load the turtles into the dinghy and carry them ashore.

"Where are they taking them?"

"There is a turtle pen in the lagoon." She smiles. "You want to show my father that you caught the turtles alive." She walks away to the plantation house and the next time he sees her, she is wearing the dark blue dress again and she looks older, and for some reason it makes him realize that with all the time they spent on the reef, sleeping together in the saloon, she never kissed him.

Gloria Fontaine

Jamie pulls the fishing net out of the tub and along the deck of the ketch, letting the loose end pile up in the cockpit. He sits on the stern of the ketch with his feet resting on a locker. The trade wind is weak, making the air heavier than usual, and even with the awning blocking some of the glare coming off the lagoon he squints as he looks for holes in the net. Someone calls him. He pushes the net off his lap and stands up. Hector is walking down from the landing. "M. Fontaine wants you."

Jamie takes off his t-shirt and puts on a short-sleeved shirt. He walks up to the landing and then past the men husking nuts. When he reaches the house he stands at the veranda steps and calls for Fontaine. At first nothing and then the scraping of a chair and Fontaine appears at the door.

"Bonjour, M. Blair. I have inspected the turtles. You are very resourceful. I think in a month or so you can pay for my share of the schooner. But first I have something else for you. One of my workers is missing. There was some carelessness and Henri was left on Hog Island." Fontaine smiles. "He must be very lonely on the island. There are only wild pigs there. Bring him back here. You can do this?"

"Yes, of course."

"Hog Island is to the east. If you go now, maybe you find it before it is dark." He turns and walks back in the house.

Jamie walks to *Selene* and readies the ketch for sea. He dumps the net back in the tub and carries it down in the forepeak. When he returns to the deck to unrig the awning, he sees Melia on the beach.

"I come with you to Hog Island."

He climbs in his dinghy and pushes it across to the beach. "Are you sure? Your father is going to know."

"It does not matter. He knows I was with you catching turtles."

"What did you tell him?"

"I told him I like sailing." She smiles. "This is true."

"Is that all?"

"He said I am wild. Out here in the islands there is not more to say."

She climbs in the dinghy and he pushes it back to the ketch. She goes below as he finishes unrigging the awning. He hauls in the stern anchor and backs the staysail. Melia takes the helm and as he secures the main anchor and sets the jib, she heads the ketch out to sea. He looks back at the landing. Arman is on the stern of the schooner.

"Captain Arman is watching us leave."

Melia shrugs and brings the ketch into the wind. Jamie goes forward to the mainmast and sets the sail. He hardens in the sheets and they tack around the southern end of the atoll.

"Do you know where Hog Island is?"

"It is there." She points to the east. "With this boat we can anchor in the lagoon. Go make coffee."

They beat to windward on the starboard tack and the ketch rises and falls over the ocean swell. In the afternoon it's time to tack to port and as the ketch comes into the wind, she slows and hangs for a moment, pitching her bow into the waves. The sails shiver until the bow passes through the wind. The jib sheet whips across the deck and Jamie hauls it in and Melia grins as the ketch picks up speed again.

Toward evening Melia sights Hog Island, a low atoll on the eastern horizon. "We sail some more and then wait for tomorrow." The daylight is almost gone when Jamie sees the white line of waves breaking on the reef. He lowers the mainsail and heaves-to under staysail and mizzen. The ketch lies quietly and he goes below to cook the yellowtail he caught earlier.

Melia is in the galley. "You make raw fish?"

"I was planning to fry it."

"Fry it tomorrow. Make raw fish now and then your pasta dish with garlic."

While they are eating, Jamie asks her if she knows Henri.

She looks up from her plate. "Seychelles is thousands of miles from one end to the other, but it is a small place. Henri is a friend of Darian. They were on the schooner when it first came to the plantation."

"Who else was on the schooner?"

"Arman. It was just the three of them."

"There should have been someone else on board, a Captain Jenkins. What happened to him?"

She shrugs. "We ask Henri when we find him." After dinner Melia goes in the forepeak and closes the door and Jamie doesn't see her again until morning.

They approach the atoll from the southwest and Melia tacks the ketch through the pass and they anchor in the lagoon. Jamie stands in the bow and surveys the atoll. It's small, about a mile across and perfectly round and covered with palm trees and shrubs and some grass. He goes below to cook breakfast. Melia says his pancakes are too thick but she eats them anyway, with strawberry jam. She finishes her plate and hands it to him to take to the galley. "We have to trick Henri. If he thinks we are here for him, he will run away. So we go on the island and catch wild pigs to bring to the plantation."

"How do we catch wild pigs?"

"Put the boat in the water and get some fish from yesterday."

Jamie rows ashore, takes a bucket with fish heads and other scraps and follows Melia along the beach. They find a path that leads into the bush and follow it until they come to a wallow with some rainwater still in it. They return to the beach. "Put the fish here. The pigs will find it."

"You want to feed the pigs fish for a few days and then put up a trap?"

"Today you are clever."

They return to the ketch and Jamie goes fishing on the lagoon. When he returns to the ketch, he sees Melia wearing her red bikini. "Did you go for a swim?"

"No. Look." Three blacktip reef sharks circle the ketch.

"Do you think the reef sharks are dangerous?"

"What do you think? They are playthings?"

Each morning Jamie leaves fish scraps at the beginning of the path to the wallow and then he cuts poles for the trap. They don't see Herni. After three days Jamie gets the net out and slices off one end and carries it and the poles to the beach. He uses the poles to hold up the top of the net and then pegs the bottom of the net to the ground. Between two poles he leaves the bottom of the net free for the pigs to enter.

Melia looks at the trap. "The pigs live in big families, two and three generations. They come when it is dark, mostly in the evening and morning. The net is not strong enough for the big ones but it may catch the small ones. Those are the ones we want."

When they return to the trap the next morning, they find the net lying in a tangled pile with three piglets in it. Jamie untangles the net and Melia holds a sail bag open as he drops the piglets in. He looks at the net. It isn't worth keeping. As they start back to the boat, Henri comes out of the bush. Melia talks to him in Creole and the worried look on his face slowly fades. He follows them to the boat.

"I told him you are Darian's friend and that we will take him to the plantation on Laurette Island. It is north of here, not far."

After dinner they all sit together in the cockpit and Henri talks quietly in Creole. Afterwards he goes to bed in the saloon. Jamie and Melia sit in the cockpit and she tells him Henri's story.

"He sailed on the schooner from Mahé with Captain Jenkins, Arman and Darian. They were for Mombasa and then Arman made Captain Jenkins sail to the Outer Islands."

"Arman took over the schooner? That's mutiny."

"Yes, it was bad. Then they put Captain Jenkins ashore on an atoll to the west of here."

"Arman marooned him? We can go look for him."

"No. That was last year and the atoll has no water. Then Arman sailed the schooner to the plantation. Herni promised not to talk but he became afraid and ran away here on Hog Island."

"What happened to Darian? Why is he at one of the copra camps?"

"He would not promise and Arman sent him there."

In the morning they set sail for Laurette Island. There is a small settlement there, a copra station, workers with their families, and an Indian store. They wait until evening and Jamie rows Henri ashore, using a light at the end of the landing to guide him. When he returns to the ketch they set sail for the south.

"Did you tell Henri not to say who brought him to the island?"

"Yes. He will say the *Marie Louise* brought him. Go feed the pigs."

The piglets are tied to the mainmast and Jamie gives them galley scraps and water. He watches them eat. They already have their sea legs. He returns to the cockpit and Melia smiles. "The pigs are happy?"

"Can't you hear them squealing for joy? Isn't that why you are smiling?"

"It is something else. I made Henri promise to go to court in Mahé when the time comes."

"You have plans?"

"I have many plans. Go make coffee."

Jamie brings two cups of coffee to the cockpit. "I looked at the chart. Why are you heading south. It's shorter to go around the north end of Heron Atoll."

"There are reefs to the north, many with no names."

Before evening a dark line of clouds appears on the eastern horizon. While Jamie is frying fish for dinner, a squall hits the ketch. It's much stronger than expected. Jamie tries to reef the main and then gives up and lowers it and heaves-to. He unties the piglets and carries them one at a time to the cockpit where there is some shelter. He goes below to the galley and takes off his wet clothes and wrings them out in the sink. The door to the forepeak is closed. He goes in the saloon and wraps himself in a blanket and lies in the lee bunk. Later in the night he wakes. The wind is still blowing and Melia is there, crawling under his blanket.

In the morning he looks at Melia as she opens her eyes and smiles. He kisses her eye and looks at her and then he kisses her other eye. He looks at her again. "Will you kiss me?"

"The sex is not enough for you?"

When he has no answer for that she crawls out of the bunk. The morning sun shining through the skylight catches her bare shoulder as she disappears into the galley.

The sea is confused but the wind has eased and after breakfast they get the ketch underway and in the afternoon they sail into the pass at Heron Atoll. No one seems to be about as Jamie watches Melia lead the three piglets away on leashes.

Jamie scrubs the deck around the mainmast and then with a bucket of water he washes the pig muck out the scuppers. He looks at the cockpit critically and then scrubs it out a second time. At least he didn't let the piglets in the saloon during the storm. As he watches the water drain out the cockpit, Hector walks down to the beach.

"M. Fontaine wants you."

Jamie goes below and washes, puts on a clean shirt and goes ashore in the dinghy. The station is unusually quiet. No one is on the schooner working and no one is in the shed husking nuts. As he approaches the house he sees Jean-Paul sitting on the steps of the veranda with his head in his arms.

"Hi, Jean-Paul."

Jean-Paul looks up and smiles. "Good boatman."

"Yes, good boatman."

Fontaine comes out to the veranda. "Bonjour M. Blair. It is unfortunate that you did not find Henri. What do you think happened to him?"

"I don't know. Perhaps he died or someone took him away."

"But you did not find a body."

"No. But with feral pigs on the island I don't think there would be a body."

"Yes, this is possible. Perhaps this is the end of it. But now there is something else. You see, no one is working. They are all afraid of this fool here, Jean-Paul, and they have run off. They think he is witched."

"How is he witched?"

"They say he dances."

"Is that all?"

"It is enough. I want you to take him to the hospital. It is an old camp on the island about two miles from here. Perhaps you have seen it?"

"Yes, the hut is visible from the lagoon."

"Good. Come with me." Fontaine walks off the veranda and leads Jamie out under the palms. "I want you to take a letter to Mahé."

"You don't want Captain Arman to take it?"

"No. This is very important and requires much discretion. You see, Captain Arman will read the letter."

"And you trust me not to read it."

Fontaine looks at Jamie sideways. "The letter is written in the French language . . . You are to deliver the letter in your person and wait for the reply. You understand?"

"Of course."

Fontaine turns and walks back toward the house. "Take the supplies to the camps and leave Jean-Paul at the hospital. The letter will be ready when you return."

Jamie watches him walk into the house and disappear through a door on the left. He looks down the passage that runs through the house and waits but Melia is nowhere about. "Come, Jean-Paul, we go to the boat." Jean-Paul stands and Jamie takes his hand and leads him to the beach next to the ketch. The boat is anchored to the shore, loaded with supplies for the camps. Jamie helps Jean-Paul into the boat and directs him to the stern. Jamie takes the dinghy to the ketch and gathers up his hat, his fishing line and a jug of water and returns to the beach. He puts the anchor in the bow of the boat and shoves off and rows up the pass to the lagoon. As soon as the wind is fair, he sets the lugsail. Jean-Paul points to the world around him, the mangroves, the herons, the clouds. Jamie holds up the fishing line.

Jean-Paul looks at it. "Fish."

Jamie hands him the fishing line and almost as soon as Jean-Paul lets the line out he catches a snapper. "That's enough fish, Jean-Paul."

"Enough fish."

When Jamie sees the hut set back under the palms, he lowers the lugsail and rows to the beach. There was once a camp here. Now the bush is growing back around the empty shed and the hut's thatched roof is leaning over so far on one side that it is resting on the ground. In the green light beyond the hut he sees a dark shape lying under a palm tree. The shape doesn't move when Jamie approaches. Bones show under the dark skin. Jamie is not sure the man is still breathing. Farther back is another man leaning against a palm tree, his head resting on his knees. The man looks up and stares, his eye red and hollow. This is the hospital.

A young man steps out of the hut. "Did you bring food?"

"Darian . . . Yes. What is this place?"

"This is where the men come to die when they cannot work."

"Fontaine calls this a hospital."

"Hell has many names."

"The man over there, lying by the tree, I think he is dying."

"Yes, and the boatman in the hut is already dead. We have to bury him."

"How? This is an atoll."

"We cover him with coral."

Jamie follows Darian into the hut and together they carry the body out in a blanket. When Jean-Paul sees the body, he falls to the ground and arches his back, his arms and legs shaking. Jamie and Darian put the body down and hurry over to him. A stick falls out of Jean-Paul's pocket and Jamie pushes Jean-Paul's chin down with the palm of his hand and inserts the stick between his teeth. They hold his arms and legs, trying to keep him from hurting himself, until suddenly he stops moving and lies on the ground looking dazed.

"What was that?"

"A seizure. I think he has epilepsy. He has to rest now."

"How do you catch it?"

"I don't know. It's something in the brain but it's not contagious. He can't give it to you."

"Leave him. We bury the boatman now." They carry the boatman over to the lee side of the island and gather coral and place it on the body until it is covered and the crabs can't get at it.

When they return to the hut, Jean-Paul is up. He has started a fire and he is cooking a fish soup and acting as if nothing has happened. He has managed to find a few vegetables for the soup and when it is ready, Jamie and Darian sit in the shade eating. Jean-Paul takes a cup to the men under the trees.

"Darian, what are you doing here?"

"I ran away."

"You mean you quit working?"

"I ran away, from the copra."

Jamie thinks about the camps and the copra and the bacca and now this, the hospital. "Fontaine makes you work here, for nothing? That's like slavery."

"No one wants to work here but we cannot leave. Bacca keeps the men quiet but they miss their families. Go now. Take the boat to the camps and bring them the rice and bacca. When you come back, I go with you to the station."

"You have a plan?"

"My plan is to go away from here."

Jamie leaves Darian and Jean-Paul and sets sail for the camps. He delivers the rice and bacca and picks up the copra and then returns to the hospital. After he lands the boat he walks over to Darian sitting under a palm.

"Darian, I've been thinking. What is your plan?"

"I will talk to my father. Maybe he takes me somewhere."

"I can take you to Mahé in my boat. Fontaine wants me to sail there when I get back to the station."

"We do this."

It's growing dark as Jamie beaches the boat next to the landing. He and Darian get in the dinghy and push it over to *Selene*. "Wait here until I come back."

"We leave now?"

"First I'm going to find Melia. She may want to come with us." Jamie shoves off in the dinghy and beaches it next to the island boat. He walks up to the landing and scans the area. Someone is smoking on the stern of the schooner. Probably Arman. He walks past the copra shed and then sees a light at the plantation house. He steps carefully up to the side of the house and looks through the window. A table with an oil lamp and a bottle of rum, Fontaine sitting in a chair holding a glass. Then Melia bursts into the room shouting in French and waving something. A letter.

She switches to English and her voice becomes harsher. "You want to sell me to this pig in Mahé."

"You will go to Mahé and there you will marry M. Hoareau. It is my wish."

"Your wish. This is not a hundred years ago. Your wish is not greater than mine." Melie sees Jamie looking through the window and smiles at him. "I think M. Blair will agree with me."

Fontaine turns to the window. "Ah, M. Blair, you look through my window?"

"I can't help it, M. Fontaine, there aren't many windows on the atoll."

"So you have wit." Fontaine looks past Jamie. "Hector, bring M. Blair here so he can entertain us." Jamie steps back and bumps into Hector who takes him by the arm and leads him into the house. As soon as Jamie enters the room, Melia runs out. She doesn't glace at him.

"M. Blair, have you been putting ideas in Melia's head? Since you are here she is rather wild."

"Perhaps I've been a catalyst. She sees me and wants the same freedom I have."

"Freedom? She is a woman, a girl. They have no ideas of freedom. They like to play a silly game. They like to say no, no, no and then they say yes and it is all settled and they are married. It is time for Melia to marry."

"Melia is right. You are living in the last century. You even treat your workers like slaves."

"What do you know about my plantation. Nothing. My workers are born slaves. It is not something I choose for them. It is in their blood, passed on from generation to generation since the Arabs first caught them. Now you come here and think this is like England and—"

"I am American."

"You interrupt me? You are becoming a nuisance. I shall be rid of you."

"What are you going to do, send me to your hospital?"

"I have a better idea. Captain Arman will take you somewhere." He looks to Hector. "Hector, take M. Blair to the storehouse. He is to stay there for now." Hector takes Jamie by the arm and leads him out of the house and into the night.

Jamie is lying on bags of copra when Hector unlocks the door to the storehouse and enters. He has brought some food and water. As he sets them down, Melia slips through the door and speaks to Hector in Creole. Hector leaves but he doesn't lock the door.

"Why did you come to the house last night? Were you looking for me? You never did that before."

"I didn't think you wanted me to come before. I came last night to take you to Mahé."

She smiles at him. "You want to rescue me, take me away in your white boat? It is not like that. I am fighting with my father. I want you to help me."

"Help you do what? Your father acts like a tyrant and everything seems to be turning upside down here. You even spoke to your father in English last night."

"In the Seychelles, English is the language of authority. This makes it a good language for anger. Tomorrow they will take you to the schooner. I think Arman wants to leave you on an atoll, like he did with the real captain. There will be you, Darian and me against Arman and his two Creoles. Hector tells me the Creoles are afraid of Arman. Perhaps that will help us." She turns to leave.

"What do you want me to do?"

"You will know when the time comes." She slips out of the storehouse and he hears the door lock.

Jamie lies in a bunk in the fo'c'sle of the schooner. The only light is from the two portholes in the hatch coaming and the twilight air is stale. They have been under sail for most of the morning, and now the schooner is hove-to, riding uneasy in a heavy sea. Darian lies in the other bunk, his back to Jamie. The hatch slides open and a voice calls for Darian. Jamie follows Darian up the ladder and as he waits for his eyes to adjust to the bright sun light, a Creole grabs his arm and leads him to the mainmast. The other Creole is in the boat that is rubbing against the side of the schooner. Arman is standing next to the helm smiling at Jamie. "We have found a place for you." He points to windward at a small, barren atoll. There are a few isolated coconut trees. The atoll in uninhabited.

"Is this where you left Captain Jenkins?"

"There are many such atolls in the Outer Islands. They are where the turtles lay their eggs and where undesirable men sit and stare at the sky." Arman looks at Darian. "You said you do not talk to anyone? How does he know of Captain Jenkins?"

Darian shrugs. "I did not talk to him."

The man in the boat begins shouting and everyone goes to the side of the schooner and looks at the water. A shark is circling. It turns toward the schooner and brushes against the boat. The man in the boat grabs the fore shrouds and quickly climbs up to the deck of the schooner. While everyone else is staring at the shark, Jamie sees Melia climb out of the aft hatch and pick up a boathook. Arman leans over the taffrail. "A bull shark, a big one." Melia steps behind Arman and as the schooner lurches, she hits him with the boathook, knocking him overboard. When Arman hits the water he starts screaming and thrashing with his arms.

Darian runs aft. "He cannot swim." He looks in the water and then dives over the taffrail. Arman is in a panic and almost drowns both of them, until Darian hits him with his fist on the side of the head, stunning him. He pulls Arman to the boat and helps him in. As Arman lies dazed in the bottom of the boat, Darian climbs in and slaps him a few times, trying to revive him.

Melia signals to Jamie. "Untie the boat and bring it aft and tie it there." She points to a sternpost. She yells at the Creoles who are staring at Arman in the bottom of the boat. They release the backed staysail, putting the schooner on the port tack. Melia turns to Jamie. "The schooner is yours. Take us back to the plantation."

"I've been in the fo'c'sle. I don't know where we are."

She points south. "The atoll is there." She takes the helm and he lets out the mainsheet and points the crew to the other sheets. He looks up at the sun. Not yet noon. He goes below to the small chartroom and finds the sexton. He takes a sun sight and then later he takes a noon sight. They are less than thirty miles northwest of Heron Atoll.

Jamie looks aft at the boat riding in the schooner's wake. "I don't think that painter will hold."

"Get a bigger rope."

Jamie goes forward and gets a mooring line from a midship locker. He ties one end to the sternpost and then pulls the boat up to the stern of the schooner. He throws the mooring line to Darian and tells him to make it fast. Darian shouts back, "Water." Jamie goes below to the galley, finds an empty bacca jug and washes it out. He fills it with water and carries it up on deck and lets it down to Darian. Then he pays out the mooring line until the boat is riding farther behind the schooner.

Jamie stands at the mainsheet holding onto the gallows. There is no cockpit on the schooner, no place to huddle behind the cabin. Then he sees that the schooner is bigger, her topsides higher, than the ketch, and the spray bursting over the bow doesn't even reach the mainmast. He looks at Melia sitting on the wooden cover over the steering-gear. She has a look of satisfaction as she heads the schooner across the open sea. It reminds him of how much she likes sailing *Selene*. Will she like sailing the schooner even more? "Why do you want to go to the plantation? Your father is there."

"Yes. That is why I go there. I fight him for the plantation."

"What do you mean?"

She smiles. "You will see."

The two Creoles sit at the break in the deck. They take turns going aft, nodding to Melia each time, and then looking at the boat in the schooner's wake.

"Why are the men looking at the boat?"

"Captain Arman made a fool of himself in the water and he has lost much of his authority. The men are looking to see if he is the same man."

Later in the afternoon, after taking a few sun sights, Jamie changes the course a little more to windward, putting the schooner on a close reach. Squalls pass ahead of them and then one hits them and the day turns dark and cold. Jamie goes below and gets Melia a foul weather jacket from a locker in the aft cabin. He gives Melia the jacket and then looks aft at the men the boat. They are huddled together in the rain. When squall passes and the sky clears, they can see the atoll. They tack into the pass. "We can't use the boat to warp in."

"We do not need the boat. Put the tires out." Jamie and the Creoles rig tires along the starboard side and Melia guides the schooner gently up to landing.

Jamie and Melia leave the schooner and hurry to the island boat on the beach. Darian joins them and Jamie pushes off and rows out to the lagoon.

"Does your father have a gun?"

"Yes, Arman too. That is why we hurry. Take us to the hospital. We will wait there."

Jamie sets the lugsail and heads the boat up the island. When they arrive at the hospital, Jean-Paul greets them and begins preparing a soup. He has spent his time at the hospital tending to the men under the trees. When the soup is ready, they sit together eating and Jamie looks at the other two. He's not sure he likes Darian but there doesn't seem to be anything between him and Melia. But not being able to speak Creole makes him uncomfortable.

"Do you think your father will come after us in the schooner's boat?"

"No. My father will be afraid to go in the boat with the Creoles and they will not come here alone. My father will wait but we have plenty of rice and fish for the next few days. Each day my father does nothing he loses more of his authority with the Creoles. When they become noisy, he will send Hector here to make an offer. Before that, you and Darian go to the camps and tell the men to come here."

In the morning Jamie and Darian sail to the camps. They give the men fish and Darian tells them Mlle. Fontaine wants to talk to them at the hospital. The men nod, cook the fish and eat before gathering their things and walking south.

When the men have all gathered at the hospital, Melia goes among them, talking to them in Creole. In the evening Jamie sits with Melia. "How do you know your father will send Hector?"

"You ask me again, how do I know? I know what my father thinks. I know what the Creoles think too. This is what my father doesn't know because he does not speak to them in Creole. My father will send Hector to speak for him. This has always been Hector's job. My father wants to turn the men against me. He will tell Hector to give the men something. Hector will say my father will give the men more bacca."

"That's it? More bacca."

"Yes, but it is not enough this time."

In the morning Hector arrives in the schooner's boat. The men gather around him on the beach and Hector talks to them. The men remain silent. Then

Melia talks to them and the men become excited. They begin to shout and some begin to dance.

Jamie turns to Darian. "What's going on"

"What Melia said. M. Fontaine gives the men more bacca, but that is all. Melia gives them their freedom. She will pay them for their work, with English pounds. Those who want to leave the plantation can leave. Most have nowhere to go. Most want to bring their families to the plantation. Now they can do this."

Melia walks over to Jamie. Her eyes are bright with excitement. "All the Creoles on the atoll are now with me. This evening you take the first boat load of men past the station to the turtle pen. Then you come back for the rest of the men."

It is dark when Jamie arrives with the second boatload of men. Melia divides the men into two groups and sends Darian with one group to take the schooner. There will be no one there but Arman. She leads the other group to the plantation house. There is a light on in the house. Jamie looks through the window. A lamp and a bottle of rum and a pistol are on the table and Fontaine is asleep in a chair. Hector is standing in the shadows of the room. Melia signals to him and he nods. She whispers to Jamie to stay and she quietly enters the house, walks up to the table and picks up the pistol. Fontaine jerks awake. She speaks to him quickly in French and when he begins to shout, she fires the gun at the ceiling. Then three of the men walk in the room and stand behind her.

Melia takes her father to the schooner. Darian is on the deck and two men are holding Arman. Melia looks at Arman and speaks to him in English. "You cannot be trusted. You and my father will stay in the forward cabin, where you had Jamie and Darian. When the *Marie Louise* comes, it will take you to Mahé."

"This is my schooner."

"Arman, you are a thief and a murderer. You will go to jail in Mahé. My father is only a thief and a fool. He will not go to jail but he is finished here."

After Fontaine and Arman are forced into the fo'c'sle, Melia turns to Jamie. "You have your schooner now. Your papers are in the house. I will give them to you tomorrow. Watch my father and Arman. I go now to pay the men and then let them celebrate." She talks to Hector and they walk toward the house with the Creoles following them.

Jamie wakes. At first he doesn't know where he is and then he remembers. The starboard bunk in the aft cabin of the schooner. He climbs on deck and then goes forward to the midship hatch and climbs below.

Gloria Fontaine

Jean-Paul is in the galley cooking. "Coffee?" Jean-Paul pours a cup of coffee and Jamie takes a sip. Jean-Paul's coffee is better than his. He goes on deck. The sun is above the clouds on the horizon but the morning is still cool. The workers are laying out the trays of copra. He steps to the port side and looks at the water in the pass. A tidal current is flowing out to sea and a turtle is swimming slowly with it. Melia let the turtles loose. He sees Hector approaching the landing. "Mlle. Fontaine wants you."

As Jamie walks across the landing he glances at the lagoon. The herons are gone and the reef flats are empty. He walks up to the plantation house and hesitates. Melia comes to the door. "Bonjour, M. Blair." Jamie looks puzzled and she laughs. "I have the plantation now. I have the responsibility. You see that."

"I see that you can't go around in a red bikini."

"No, not now and probably not ever again. That is in the past. Here are your papers. What do you plan with *Selene?*"

"I'll leave her here for you."

"That is generous. It is a good boat. I will give you a load of copra to take with you."

"So you know I will leave."

She smiles. "I have always known that."

"I'm going to miss you."

"Yes, it is part of saying good-bye. That is how it is in the islands." She is still smiling as she walks back into the plantation house.

Jamie watches Darian sitting on a platform rigged under the stern of the schooner. He is painting a new name on her transom. *Stella Maris,* San Francisco. When Darian is finished he hands up the paint and the brushes to Jamie and climbs over the stern to the deck. Together they unrig the platform and carry it forward and stow it in the boat. "Come down to the galley. Jean-Paul will make us some coffee." They sit with their coffee at the table in the main cabin. The sunlight shining through the skylight slants across the cabin.

"We take Jean-Paul back to Aldabra. It is foolish of my father to take him away from there."

"You are going to come with me? I thought you wanted to go to Mahé. You are a witness to your father's mutiny and the marooning of Captain Jenkins."

"No. I go with you to Mombasa. I do not go to the court and speak against my father. Henri will do that." The light fads in the cabin as dark clouds slide in front of the sun.

A squall passes over the atoll and when the sky clears a schooner appears in the offing. *Marie Louise.* She heaves-to and sends a boat ashore. Melia comes out to the landing and tells the men in the boat to bring *Marie Louise* into the pass and moor alongside the other schooner. The wind gusts as *Marie Louise* slowly tacks into the pass. She falls off and comes up into the wind. The crew throw the lines and Jamie catches them and the two schooner moor side-by-side. Captain Jack Carter crosses over to the landing and Melia falls into his arms and kisses him.

Stella Maris

The wind blows out of Africa and sweeps across the island of Cape Verde, lifting dirt off the land and spreading it over the bay. Jamie stands at the foremast of *Stella Maris* feeling the fine grit under his bare feet. A gust of wind hits the schooner and she snubs at her anchor. He goes aft to the compass and checks his position. The anchor is dragging. He goes forward and lets out more chain. He could move closer to the town that sits at the end of the bay. Maybe later. He begins throwing buckets of water on the deck and washes the grit out the scuppers. Down at the mouth of the bay a large schooner beats in against the wind. A local trading schooner with a broken back and rusty chain-plates. She has a large crew and after she drops her anchor, the crew puts a boat over the side and the captain climbs in and sits aft with the ship's compass in his lap as four men row him ashore.

Later in the morning two men row out to *Stella Maris* in an open fishboat. The people of Saint Vincent are poor and the men barter for clothes. Jamie holds up a shirt for a lobster and three eggs, pointing to the items in the boat as the men smile and chat in the local Creole. He cooks the lobster for lunch and as he eats, the awning over the aft cabin rips and snaps in the wind. Both of the forward grommets have torn out. He takes the awning down, dropping it in the aft cabin, and then he checks the forward awning over the main cabin and takes it down as well. He doesn't finish the lobster. It reminds him of Nicobar where he ate lobsters every day until their rich flesh no longer appealed to him. In the afternoon he sits in the aft cabin with the sun shining through the skylight, the awning in his lap as he repairs its torn corners. No one else is on board the schooner.

The next morning his dinghy is floating upside down under the stern of the schooner. The wind flipped it over in the night. He goes to the compass and checks his position. The anchor is holding. He pulls the dinghy up to the taffrail and turns it over and then climbs in and bails out the rest of the water. He climbs back on deck and looks forward. At the head of the bay, Arnoldo is heading toward the schooner in an open boat. He has his oars out but he lets the wind drive him down the bay. He comes alongside, stands up and grabs the taffrail. "Morning Captain."

"Morning Arnoldo, any news?"

"A good crew is hard to find."

"I've been waiting here a month."

Arnoldo smiles proudly. "Now I bring a man and a cook."

"Is the cook a man too?"

Arnoldo stops smiling. "You think I bring a woman on a ship?" He pushes off and mans the oars. "You ready, we leave tomorrow." He rows back to the town, pulling hard against the wind.

Three days later Arnoldo brings out the new crew to the schooner and Jamie meets them as they climb aboard carrying small canvas bags. "Captain, here is Miguel and here is our cook, Paulo." They stow their bags in the fo'c'sle and then return to the deck and hoist the mainsail and foresail. The sails shiver as Arnoldo operates the anchor winch. The cook Paulo goes below again and flakes down the chain and Miguel readies the davit to haul the anchor aboard. The crew work well together, with only a few quiet words from Arnoldo. The schooner begins making sternway until the anchor is lashed on deck and the staysail is backed and then she swings past the trading schooner and heads out the bay.

Arnoldo walks aft and stands next to Jamie. "We make Bonaire in three weeks."

"First we stop in Barbados."

"No, no. Barbados is no good for us. We go straight to Bonaire. It is in the ship's articles."

"What ship's articles?"

"Here." Arnoldo taps the side of his head and smiles.

Jamie sits at the helm watching the sails and the night sky. The sails are full with the northeast trade wind coming over the starboard quarter, and the sky is clear and moonless and filled with stars spread from horizon to horizon. Arnoldo comes out the midship hatch and walks aft. "Evenin' Captain. Good sailing tonight."

"Yes. We're making seven knots."

There's a sudden thud. Something hits the mainsail and they both look forward. Arnoldo calls out in Creole and moments later the cook comes running aft with a bucket. The cook climbs on the cabin top and begins searching. There's another thud. The cook picks up something and puts it in the bucket.

Stella Maris

Arnoldo turns to Jamie. "Flying fish for breakfast, Captain."

In the morning the flying fish appear to windward, their silver sides catching the sunlight as they launch themselves over the waves. Arnoldo points to them. "Give me a hook, Captain. Something is chasing them." Jamies goes below and gets out a fishline from the lazaret. Arnoldo lets out the fishline as the flying fish continue to glide over the waves, outpacing the schooner. Arnoldo hooks a fish and slowly hauls it in. He grins as he holds it up to show Jamie. A wahoo.

When the trade wind fails in the mid-Atlantic, Arnoldo sends Miguel aloft to set the topsail and then Arnoldo and Miguel rig the fishman staysail and hoist it up to the top of the masts. Jamie watches from the helm as the sails fill and the schooner picks up maybe half a knot. He hasn't set either of the light-weather sails before. He wasn't even sure how to set the fisherman staysail. The wind picks up as they sail south of Barbados and the flying fish begin to accompany them again, with a few of them landing on deck at night. It's almost five weeks before they round the northern end of Bonaire Island and sail in its lee, protected from the sea but not the wind. They anchor in a wide bay in front of a resort with bungalows spread along the beach. Off the stern of the schooner is Little Bonaire

Island, low and uninhabited. As soon as the sails are furled, the crew goes below for their small bags. Jamie waits at the mainmast until Arnoldo returns to the deck. "We go now, Captain. Do not worry. We come back soon and sail with you to Panama." He grins. "Who knows, maybe we sail with you all the way to America." Arnoldo and the other two men climb in the dinghy and row ashore, leaving Jamie on the schooner. He watches them go and then rigs the awnings before swimming ashore to fetch his dinghy.

The sun rises above the white clouds that ring the horizon and the wind blows across the low island, carrying sand out over the bay. Jamie throws a bucket of water on the deck and washes the grit out the scuppers. When he looks up, a thirty-six-foot sloop sails into the bay and drops her anchor. *Escape,* Miami. Four people onboard, one couple sitting in the cockpit, the other couple working the boat. A charter boat. The skipper of *Escape* rows the charter couple ashore and carries their luggage up to the main building of the resort. It's a resort for scuba divers and the charter couple haven't brought any diving gear.

In the late afternoon as the sun hangs in the west over Little Bonaire, Jamie rows ashore and walks up to the resort. Harry is behind the bar.

"Hello, Jamie, still waitin' for your crew to come back?"

"How are you doing, Harry. Give me a Red Stripe and put it on my tab."

"You don't have a tab."

"You can start one."

Harry opens a bottle of beer and slides it down the bar. "On the house."

"You do any sailing?"

"How do you think I got here? I sailed from San Diego on a ketch called *Sinister*, a stupid name for a boat. Everybody ended up yelling at everybody else on board, so I left. And if you are asking if I want to crew on your schooner, I like it here at the bar just fine."

Jamie sips his beer. "Have you seen the couple that came in on the charter boat?"

"No. They order drinks sent to their bungalow. They didn't even come into the dining room for lunch."

"What do you make of that?"

"What do I make of it? I don't know. Maybe they just got married and want a lot of privacy, you know."

"If that's so, why are they spending time on a charter boat. Not much privacy there."

"That's what Captain Dave says. They got off his boat here because there wasn't enough privacy, there wasn't even enough room for all their suitcases. Look, here comes Captain Dave now."

Jamie turns to see the skipper of *Escape* walk toward the bar. Harry introduces them and they shake hands.

"Harry tells me your charter left you."

Captain Dave looks at Jamie and then turns to Harry. "Give me a beer."

Jamie looks at his bottle of beer. "Yeah, I know it's none of my business. I was just making conversation with Harry."

Captain Dave turns back to Jamie. "It may be your business. Davenport is talking about chartering your schooner. I don't like to complain about my guests but I think maybe I should give you a heads up. He's a bit strange. The girl is okay. She helps Sally in the galley and puts her clothes away where they belong."

"What kind of strange?"

"He comes aboard with a lot of suitcases and complains about the lack of space. Then he wants to sail around Los Roques Archipelago, looking for his lost brother, he says, but every time we anchor somewhere he doesn't want to go ashore. That's the strange part."

"Doesn't he cause any real problems?"

"Let me put it this way, if you take him on, be sure he buys his own liquor."

The morning sun is still low as Jamie climbs out the aft hatch and goes forward and turns off the riding light. He looks over the bow before diving in the water and swimming down along the anchor chain until he can see the anchor. Back on board he goes below to the galley and makes his morning coffee and then takes his cup on deck and sits on the box over the steering gear. The wind gusts and he can see sand being swept off the land. Some of it falls on the deck of the schooner. He gets out the bucket and washes the grit out the scuppers. The bay, the island, the wind and the sand, the world doesn't seem to change. The skipper of *Escape* raises his anchor, while his crew, probably his wife, starts the engine and heads the sloop out the bay. They set the sails and tack into the trade wind before disappearing around the northern end of the island. As the sun rises higher, the tourists come out with their diving gear and the dive instructor leads them up the beach to the rocks where the resort advertises an underwater grotto.

In the afternoon Jamie rows ashore and walks up the beach to the resort. As he enters the bar, Harry signals to him.

"Mr. Davenport wants to talk to you. He's sitting on the veranda of his bungalow, number nine, at the end of the row."

Jamie walks out to the patio. A young woman is swimming in the pool. She's wearing a dark blue one-piece swimsuit with a low-cut back. He watches her swims laps with her blond hair flowing behind her. She's a good swimmer. He turns away and walks down the row of bungalows to number nine. The bungalow has a small veranda, half hidden behind a bush of pink bougainvillea. "Mr. Davenport? I'm Jamie Blair, owner of the schooner in the bay."

"I've been waiting for you. Sit down."

Jamies sits and waits as Davenport swirls the ice in his drink. He's an older man, probably late fifties, with thinning hair and sagging skin under the eyes.

"Harry at the bar said you wanted to talk to me."

Davenport takes a sip. "My daughter and I have left the *Escape*. We found the boat unsuitable for our needs, and now we are looking for a bigger boat to charter. Are you interested?"

"Yes, if the conditions are right."

"Good. But first I would like my daughter to have a look at your boat. We have conditions as well, you see. She will be available tomorrow morning. After she has seen your boat, we will talk again." He goes back to swirling his drink. Jamie stands and walks back through the patio. The girl in the dark blue swimsuit climbs out of the pool and starts drying herself off with a towel. Her skin glows in the sunlight as the water drips off her and pools at her feet.

"Miss Davenport?"

She looks up, holding the towel in front of her. "Claire. Is that your schooner in bay?"

"Yes, I'm Jamie. Your father said he wants you to inspect her."

"Inspect her? Does she have rats and cockroaches?"

"No rats and the cockroaches only come out at night."

She smiles. "Do you want me to inspect your boat at night?"

"I think that's a personal question. I'll row you out tomorrow morning."

Jamie eats his oatmeal and then takes his coffee on deck and watches the sun rise over the island. When the sun is above the clouds on the horizon, he rows ashore and goes into the bar. It's still too early and no one is there. He goes out to the patio and sits in one of the deckchairs and waits. Claire arrives wearing a white blouse and shorts, her blond hair tied back.

Jamie stands. "Good morning. Shall we go out to the schooner or would you like coffee first?"

"I've had coffee. Let's go out to your boat."

They walk down to the beach and he pushes the dinghy in the water and holds it steady as she climbs in. "Sit in the stern."

"I usually sit in the bow."

"Yes, when there are three people. But there's only the two us now."

She sits and he climbs in and ships the oars. "You want me to sit here so you can watch me?"

He starts rowing. "I have to watch you. As soon as you step in my dinghy I become responsible for you."

"You make it sound so impersonal."

"Really? The sky, the sea and the wind are impersonal. My dinghy is personal."

"And your schooner? Is it personal too?"

"She's very personal, that's why she's a she."

"Perhaps she's too personal for us to charter."

"I'll introduce you to her, tell her you are a special person and then she won't mind your bare feet on her deck."

She looks past Jamie to the schooner. "When you introduce me to her tell her I thinks she's beautiful." She doesn't need any help climbing up the boarding ladder. He follows her and ties the dinghy aft. When he looks up, she is standing by the helm, frowning.

"There's no cockpit."

"She's a yacht but designed like a work boat. You can sit or lie on the cabin top. You're higher off the water than on *Escape*. It doesn't usually get wet aft of the mainmast."

"May I go below?"

"Of course." She climbs down the companionway, looks left into the chartroom and then walks into the aft cabin. "The aft cabin has its own head and sink, and the engine room separates it from the rest of the boat."

"Will Morris and I have use of this cabin?"

"Yes, of course. I'll move my gear forward." They climb back on deck and walk forward.

"And this is the engine room?"

"Yes." He lifts the hatch and she looks in. There's very little light and the engine seems to squat at the bottom of a well. He closes the hatch and they walk past the mainmast and climb down. "This is the galley and on the starboard side is the head." They walk into the main cabin with a folding table in the center. The table seats six.

"And this is the saloon?"

"Yes. Forward is the fo'c'sle, the crew's quarters."

"Should I look in there?"

"Not unless you want to. It's not a part of the boat you will be using."

They climb back on deck. "There's a lot of room but it doesn't seem very comfortable."

"Her comfort is in the way she sails. She's very easy at sea."

She looks up at the masts. "It must be exciting to sail her." She points to the main crosstrees. "I would like to climb up there."

"Go ahead."

"You don't think I can do it?"

"I don't know what you can do."

She pulls herself into the shrouds and starts climbing up the ratlines. Halfway up she looks down and smiles and then she climbs the rest of the way. She stands on the crosstrees with one arm around the topmast as the wind whips the collar of her blouse. She looks at the world below. "Marvelous. I can see all the way across the island." She climbs down carefully and then springs onto the deck. "Have you been up there? The world looks immense. I'll tell Morris we have to take her."

"I should add that there's no shower or refrigeration on board."

"Really? Even *Escape* has refrigeration."

"*Escape* is a charter boat. Paying guests expect cold drinks."

"I don't think Morris will like that and he's the one to decide."

"I probably should have told Mr. Davenport that at the beginning."

Jamie brings the dinghy alongside the schooner. Claire hesitates. "Do you mind if I row?"

"No, but you'll be rowing against the wind." Jamie climbs in first and holds the dinghy steady for her. He pushes off and Claire ships the oars. Jamie starts to tell her to roll her hands forward on the backstroke but then he sees she is already doing it. "You've rowed a boat before."

"Yes, but not a boat as sluggish as this one." She beaches the dinghy and they climb out and stand on the sand facing each other.

"I don't think Morris will charter the schooner but I know I would."

Jamie smiles. "I'm looking for crew. You're welcome to join me for Panama."

"Really? I may take you up on it." She steps forward and kisses him lightly and then she runs barefoot up the beach to the resort.

Jamies sits at the helm drinking his afternoon coffee and watching a frigatebird swoop over the water, fishing the bay. Claire, an American girl. Why did she kiss him? Melia made him feel that kissing is reserved for lovers and now Claire makes him feel kissing is as natural as saying hello or good-bye. A world apart. He throws the rest of his coffee in the bay and rows ashore and walks into the resort. He looks at the patio but doesn't see Davenport, so he goes to the bar.

"Hi Harry. Does Davenport come out about this time?"

"Yeah, I already served him a couple of drinks on his veranda. I'm making another rum and coke for him now."

"You want me to bring it to him?"

"What, and pocket my tip?"

Jamie walks out to the patio and watches Claire swimming in the pool until she notices him. He waves and then walks along the row of bungalows, passing a line of tourists coming back from their dive. They seem excited about something. Jamie walks up to Davenport sitting at the small table with an empty glass.

"Afternoon, Mr. Davenport."

"Ah, yes." He tries to swirl his drink and then notices that it's empty. "I don't think your boat is suitable for us." Harry arrives with a fresh drink. "It's about time." Harry places the glass on the table and Davenport reaches for it and takes a sip. He looks up at Jamie and Harry standing before him. He ignores Harry. "You shouldn't try to pass your boat off as a yacht."

"She has a lot of room for suitcases. I thought that was the main requirement." Davenport frowns and turns away and Jamie and Harry leave together.

"Don't know what that was about but you cost me a tip."

"Sorry. He doesn't want to charter my schooner. I wanted to see what he had to say."

"He didn't say anything."

"Yes, that says a lot."

Jamie climbs down into the engine room and starts the generator to charge his batteries. He decides to clean the fuel filter on the auxiliary engine. He dislikes the smell of diesel and working in the engine room always puts him in a bad mood. When he is finished he climbs out of the engine room and looks at the sky. The wind has died down. He gets out his fishing gear, puts it in the dinghy and rows around to the lee side of Little Bonaire. The water is clear and the brightly colored coral reminds him of sugar candy. He opens a can of corn and throws a spoonful in the water. Small fish nibble at the yellow kernels as they sink to the orange and purple coral. He lowers his fishline and waits. Nothing. He throws another spoonful of corn and catches a yellowtail snapper. He throws more corn until the can is empty and he has four snappers. He rows back into the bay and up to the resort and carries the string of fish to the kitchen. The cook takes the fish and later the manager comes to the bar and gives Jamie twenty dollars.

"Harry, I want to pay my bar tab."

"You don't have a bar tab." He opens a beer. "On the house."

He sits at the bar drinking his beer and listening to the tourists talk about their day diving. As the sun is setting a man comes into the bar and joins the other tourists. "They just arrested some guy in one of the bungalows." Jamie gets up and walks out to the patio. There's no one in the pool. He looks down the row of bungalows. People are going in and out of number nine, one of them in uniform. He walks out to the parking lot. Davenport is sitting in the backseat of a black car and a uniformed policeman is standing next to it. He doesn't see Claire. Back in the bar the tourists are talking about the arrest but nobody knows anything. Jamie waits around, walking out to the patio and looking down the row of bungalows, until it turns dark and then he rows out to the schooner. He rigs his riding light and then walks aft. Something slaps the side of the schooner. Claire is in the water holding on to the boarding ladder.

"Do you need any help?"

"No, just let me rest a moment." She climbs up ladder and stands on deck, dripping in her swimsuit. It takes a moment for Jamie to react.

"Come below and I'll get you a towel."

"I'm dripping wet."

"It's okay. The schooner is used to wet." She follows him into the aft cabin and he hands her a towel. "You may find something to put on in that drawer." He points. "I'll go make some tea." He doesn't ask if she wants any tea. He doesn't want any tea himself but he can't stay in the cabin while she dresses. When he returns with two cups of black tea she is sitting on the port bunk wearing one of his t-shirts and a pair of his shorts. She has her knees pulled up with her feet resting on the edge of the bunk. Her wet hair clings to her face and her clothes are too big for her. She looks like an innocent child.

"At the resort they are saying your father has been arrested."

"I know."

"He's not your father, is he?"

"No, I met him in Port of Spain and he offered me some money to play the part of his daughter for a while. I think he was using me as some kind of blind."

"Do you know why he was arrested?"

"I think it's the suitcases. He carries them everywhere. They are probably full of money. Now I'm afraid of being caught up in whatever he did."

"Well, if you left your clothes in the bungalow, they will be looking for you."

She gets up from the bunk and walks over to him and puts her arms around his neck. "I was hoping I could stay here, just for a while."

"You can stay here as long as you like."

"I was hoping you would say that." She kisses him lightly and moves back to the bunk.

Early the next morning, Jamie rows ashore and walks to Davenport's bungalow. He knocks and then tries the door. It's locked. He's thinking of breaking in and getting Claire's clothes when a large man in a yellow Hawaiian shirt approaches. "What are you doing here?"

"I'm looking for Mr. Davenport."

"What do you want to see him about?"

"Why do you want to know?"

"Davenport's real name is Meyers. He stole something and I'm here to get it back."

"How did you find him?"

"It was easy. He was going around with a lot of suitcases."

"Did you recover the money?"

"Look, I'm the detective so let me ask the questions. Why do you want to see Meyers?"

"I'm Paul Bunyan. I chop down trees."

"Okay, here's my card." He takes out a business card and hands it to Jamie.

Jamie reads it. "Murphy and Doyle, Detectives." He looks up at the detective's sunburnt head. "Which one are you?"

"I'm Doyle."

Jamie hands the card back. "I'm the owner of the schooner anchored in the bay." He points between the bungalows. "Davenport wants to charter her."

"Does he. And where does he want to go?"

"He wants to go to Los Roques Archipelago. He said he is looking for his lost brother."

"He doesn't have a lost brother. Do you know the girl that was with him?"

"I've seen her swimming in the pool a few times. I usually go to the bar in the afternoon for a beer."

The detective stares at Jamie. "It's a little early to be calling on someone."

"It's the tropics. You get up early here. Haven't you noticed that?"

"I want to come out and take a look at your boat."

"You think you can get a search warrant here?"

"It's like that is it?" Doyle stares at Jamie, trying to make him flinch. Jamie smiles and Doyle lets out his breath. "I can deal with most people but a smart-ass really burns me up." He walks toward the bar.

Jamie rows back to the schooner and goes in the aft cabin. Claire is lying in the port bunk reading the schooner's logbook. "I have a few novels if you want some lighter reading."

"This is fascinating. You got the schooner in the Seychelles and sailed it here? How did you get to the Seychelles?"

"I'll tell you some other time. There's an American detective at the resort. He claims he tracked down Davenport, or Meyers as he calls him."

"Just as I thought. Morris is into some real trouble. Do you think the detective will come looking for me?"

"He wants to search the schooner. I told him no but he's going to persist."

"Can you stop him?"

"Yes, for a while at least, but that will only make him suspicious."

"Can't we just leave? Go somewhere else. You said you want to go to Panama."

"I need a crew to work the schooner."

She sits up and swings her feet to the deck. "You must have had a crew to get here. What happened to them?"

"I had three guys from the Cape Verde Islands. They were the best crew I ever had. When they got off here they said they would come back but so far they haven't."

"Do you think they'll come back?"

"Not any longer. I think they left for Bazil."

She looks down at her feet and then up at him again, smiling. "What does it take to sail this boat? Maybe you can find someone at the resort who will come with us." He looks at her smile. Sunlight shines in the cabin and he can see the blue of her eyes, a dark blue like her swimsuit. He can't see behind the eyes.

In the afternoon the dive instructor brings the detective out to the schooner in the dive boat. As he throttles back, Jamie shouts from the main shrouds. "You can't come aboard." The boat slides alongside and its engine hums.

Doyle stands up in the boat. "Look, let me tell you something. There's a ten-thousand-dollar reward for finding the girl that was with Meyers."

"Ten-thousand for finding the girl or for finding the missing money?"

"You know where the girl is?"

"She seems to have gone missing."

"What are you up to?"

"What does it look like? I'm getting ready to sail."

"You're hiding that girl. That makes you an accessory."

"An accessory to what?"

Doyle signals to the dive instructor to take him back to shore.

Jamie goes below. Claire is standing in the middle of the cabin. "Why is he looking for me?"

Jamie looks at her for a moment. "You said Davenport had a lot of money. What do you think happened to it?"

"I think he buried it on one of the keys in Los Roques. He carried a suitcase with him when he went ashore. Once he came back without it."

"Captain Dave said Davenport didn't leave the boat. He said it was strange that he wanted to find his brother but didn't look for him."

"That's an exaggeration. Morris often went ashore. It's just that sometimes he didn't want to and Captain Dave made an issue of it."

"Do you think you can find that key again, where he buried the suitcase?"

"Do you know how many keys there are out there? Over three hundred."

"If you don't have the money, why are you hiding?"

"What do you think will happen to me? They will think I know where it is." She laughs. "It's like pirates and buried treasure. Maybe Morris drew a map."

Jamie gets a sail bag out of the fo'c'sle and tears an old awning in half and puts one half in the sail bag. He goes to the aft cabin. "What does your suitcase look like?"

"It's small and black. It has a red twine on the handle. Are you going to get it for me?"

"I'm going to try. Is there anything you need from town? I'm going in to buy some supplies."

"Can you get me a toothbrush?"

"Sure. Anything else?"

"Get a crewmember. Maybe they sell them along with other supplies."

He puts the sail bag in the dinghy and rows ashore. At the bar Harry gives him a beer. "Still no crew? What's in the bag? Your laundry?"

"A sail I'm trying to get repaired. Do you ever take any time off?"

"What do you mean? You still want me to crew for you?"

"What about a few days in Panama?"

"I get a few days off next week, then I'll go out with the dive instructor and check out that grotto everyone talks about."

Jamie sips his beer and watches the manager's office. When the manager goes out to the kitchen, Jamie takes the sail bag and slips into the office. Claire's suitcase is behind the desk with Davenport's suitcases. He takes the awning out of the sail bag and then opens her suitcase and dumps her clothes in the bag. He puts the awning in the suitcase and closes it and then ties the mouth of the bag. He walks out of the office and takes a taxi into town.

A shaft of sunlight shines through the skylight and lands on Claire's feet. She has painted her toes dark red and she is wearing her white blouse and shorts. She looks young but no longer a child.

"What were you doing in Port of Spain?"

"Are you going to play detective now?"

"I like a good story."

"I was traveling with a boyfriend and I left him there. I was stranded in a hotel near the airport. I didn't have much money and I didn't have a plane ticket back to the States. That's why I agreed to Morris's proposal."

"Do you often leave boyfriends in foreign ports?"

She makes a grimace. "I'm attracted to men with lots of money and good manners but they always turn out to be jerks of the worst kind, selfish, egoistical, and narcissistic, all the features of the perfect male."

"I can take you to San Francisco but not as a passenger. You'll have to crew."

"You want me to cook?"

"No, I can do that. You'll have to stand watch, steer a compass course and keep an eye on the horizon. Have you done any sailing?"

"Just day sailing on a thirty-foot sloop. It had a cockpit and a tiller."

"Good, then you have a feel for it."

The bunks in the aft cabin are under the deck. Jamie strings a small line at the edge above the bunks.

"What are you doing?"

"Look in the bag on the other bunk. I bought some cloth in town. There're some hooks and needles and thread in there as well."

Claire looks in the bag. "You want me to sew curtains?"

"I need to go into town again for more supplies. I'm going to lock the hatch. If anything happens you can climb out the skylight."

Jamie rows to the resort and walks into the bar. He doesn't see any tourists.

"Hi Harry, where is everyone?"

"The dive instructor quit. He got a better job in the Florida Keys. Now the manager wants me to take some time off."

"My offer to sail to Panama still stands."

"You got any other crew?"

"Just the two of us. With this wind it's a six-day run."

"I'll let you know."

Jamie goes into town and buys eggs and fresh fruit. On his way back he stops at the bar again. Harry isn't there and when he turns to go he sees Doyle sitting in a deckchair out on the patio. Jamie walks out to him. "I've got something for you. It looks like Davenport buried the money on one of the islands out in Los Roques."

Doyle looks up at him. "How do you know that?"

"Talk to Captain Dave of *Escape*. He can tell you where he took Davenport."

"It sounds like a wild goose chase."

"Yeah, you can probably get more done sitting here in the sun."

"What if I want to charter your boat?"

"You ever do any sailing?"

"I'm hiring you for that."

"Ok. Five-hundred dollars deposit and one-hundred dollars a day with a one-week minimum."

"Are you trying to jerk me around? That's more than hotel prices."

"Hotels can't take you anywhere."

"Huh."

"Something else. The top of your head is lobster red."

The aft cabin is quiet in the afternoon except for the awning flapping in the wind now and then. Jamie stands next to Claire as they look at the curtains. "Get in the bunk and turn on the bunk light."

"Can you see through them?"

"No. The curtains look good. I'm going to pick up Harry. As soon as I bring him back to the schooner, we'll get underway."

She pushes the curtain aside and sits with her feet on the deck. "I'm nervous."

"It's the waiting. Once we are at sea you will feel better."

"Do you think Harry will give me away?"

"Ten-thousand dollars is a lot of money for someone who doesn't have any."

"It's not a lot of money for you?"

"I think you're worth more than that. Stay in the port bunk when he is on watch."

"I wish I could help."

"After Panama."

Jamie rows ashore and walks up to the resort. Harry is sitting on the customer's side of the bar with his seabag.

"Hi Harry. You ready to go?"

"All ready skipper." He shoulders his seabag and they walk to the dinghy and Jamie rows out to the schooner. "When do you want to leave."

"We leave now. Put your bag in the fo'c'sle while I start the engine." They raise the anchor and swing it on board with the davit. Jamie goes aft and powers the schooner out of the bay. When they are clear of Little Bonaire, Harry takes the gaskets off the sails and together they raise the mainsail, sweating out the sag in the luff. They set the foresail together and then

Harry sets the headsails. Jamie heads the schooner north with the wind on the starboard beam. They have to clear Aruba before heading west.

The sky is a pale blue and the schooner heads toward a horizon bordered with white clouds. The waves are long and smooth and they raise the schooner up and let her down as they pass under her. To windward the sea is a dark blue except where the crest breaks and white foam slides down their face. Jamie lets out the logline and watches the gauge on the taffrail log as it starts to rotate. Seven knots.

When the sun sets and they begin to lose the light, Jamie eases the sheets until the wind is on the quarter. He doesn't want to run dead before the wind in the heavy sea. Tomorrow they will tack and have the wind on the other quarter. "Take the helm, Harry, and I'll go cook up dinner."

"What are we having?"

"Potatoes and eggs."

"I can eat anything."

Jamie stands in the galley, swaying with the motion of the schooner as she rises up and runs down the waves. When he finishes eating, he stuffs a large thermos with potatoes and scrambled eggs, leaves a plate of food for Harry and climbs on deck. As he heads aft with his knees bent, he hugs the thermos with one arm and uses his free hand to grab the handrail on the cabin top. "I'll take the first watch, Harry."

"Where's my dinner?"

"It's on the stove. I'll call you at midnight."

The night sky is clear and ahead he can see Sirus following behind Orion and overhead a halfmoon. He looks aft and sees the fag-end of the logline whirling. The schooner is making eight to nine knots. Jamie calls down the hatch to Claire. She comes to the companionway and he stands in the steering well and hands her the thermos. She opens it and looks in.

"I guess there isn't any room for coffee."

"I'll bring you some coffee when I get off watch."

She spoons the food onto a plate and sits on the lee bunk to eat.

"The eggs and potatoes taste delicious."

"It's the sea air, the cook's secret sauce."

When she is finished eating she washes up and then stands on the companionway ladder with just her head above the deck. The schooner rolls as the swells pass under her and Claire's face rolls with it, in and out of the moonlight. He looks from the compass to the set of the sails to the horizon and back to her face.

"What do you see?"

"I see that we're make good time. This should be a short run."

"How long have you been at sea?"

"Almost four years. I've had *Stella Maris* for almost two now. Before that I sailed on the ketch *Selene.* I sailed her for thirty-eight days from Nicobar Island, just north of Sumatra, to the Seychelles. That was my longest run. I should be back in San Francisco now but I've had a series of crew problems. Now there's Harry. I'll probably lose him in Panama."

"It's just as well, don't you think?"

"He's a good crew. It's hard to say if we'll find someone as good."

Jamie hauls in the logline before they tack. Harry goes forward and they harden in the sheets and the schooner heads into the heavy sea. When the sails shiver and the sheet blocks begin to hammer the deck, Jamie has to shout into the wind. "Back the staysail. Use the block and tackle with the hook." The bow pitches into the waves and the sea washes over the deck and runs down to the break at the mainmast. The schooner seems to hesitate for a moment and then her bow passes through the wind and she falls off on the port tack. Harry eases the sheets forward and walks aft to take the helm.

Jamie goes below to prepare dinner. He cooks beans and bakes cornbread and brings the thermos with Claire's food to the helm. "Your foods is on the stove, Harry."

"Am I gonna have the midwatch all the time?"

"We can do a dogwatch tomorrow and switch."

Harry goes forward and Jamie hands Claire the thermos. After she eats she stands again on the companionway ladder. They don't talk for a while. A night watch at sea is intimate and often leads to long silences. He looks forward but there is nothing to see, no lights on the dark horizon. The pressure of the wind, the roll of schooner, and the clatter of the rigging tells him everything he needs to know. He glances at the pale face in the companionway.

"Why do you look at me? Do I remind you of someone?"

"No, just the opposite. You make me forget someone."

"Someone you love?"

"Yes, but she preferred someone else."

"He had a sailboat too?"

"He had a bigger one, an eighty-foot trading schooner. And he spoke French and Creole and he was there first, long before me, probably a childhood sweetheart."

"She must have liked you in some way."

"She liked me well enough but I was just a friend, someone to pass the time with. She wore a red bikini. It was the first one I ever saw."

"You prefer red to blue?"

"Blue looks good on you. You should try on a bikini of the same color."

"And let my bellybutton show?"

"It's probably worth showing."

"Do you think of me naked?"

"I haven't seen you naked." She steps back off the ladder and into the cabin and starts to undress. In the darkness of the cabin she is just a shadow, a naked shadow swaying to the roll of the schooner.

Jamie gets off watch and climbs down to the chartroom to write the log. Sometimes he sleeps in the bunk behind the chart table but it's built athwartships, making it uncomfortable when the schooner is heeling over. He goes into the aft cabin. Claire is in the port bunk with her back to him. He sits on the edge of the bunk and puts his hand on her shoulder and then up to the back of her neck and caresses it gently. She makes a noise that suggests pleasure and he moves his hand under the blanket and caresses her bare shoulder and then he moves the blanket aside and bends down and kisses her shoulder. She turns to him and he slides into the bunk.

After taking the noon sight Jamie calculates their position and then he goes on deck and relieves Harry. "We're making over two-hundred miles noon-to-noon."

"I've never seen anything like this. This is perfect sailing conditions." Harry goes forward and Claire comes to the companionway and Jamie smiles at her.

"What happened last night. Did I ravish you or did you seduce me?"

"I've been waiting for you. You are a little timid but last night was nice."

Jamie sights the light at the end of the Colón breakwater. The night is overcast as they heave-to under foresail and staysail. Jamie climbs down to the chartroom and Harry follows him. "Where's the girl?"

Claire appears at the doorway. "I'm here. What do you want?"

"I want ten-thousand dollars."

Jamie looks at Harry. "Did Doyle put you up to this?"

"You know, that wasn't very clever with the suitcase. He found that old bit of canvass you left there right away."

"What do you plan to do?"

"Tomorrow we go in and anchor off Colón and I go ashore. That's all you need to know."

Jamie pushes past Harry. "We go in now." He climbs on deck and walks forward on the windward side.

Harry follows him. "What are you talking about. Wait until morning. It's too dark to go in now."

Jamie ignores him. He lifts the anchor off the deck with the davit and cats it, leaving it ready to drop. Harry refuses to help him set the mainsial. He calls Claire and hands her the tail end of the throat halyard. "Keep the line taunt." Together they raise the mainsail. He goes forward and lowers and furls the foresail. Harry continues to follow him around, complaining about going into port at night. Jamie eases the sheets of the staysail and mainsail and tells Claire to head the schooner toward the light on the end of the breakwater. The entrance of the breakwater slowly opens up and when it's due south, Jamie tacks to port. The water is calm and the schooner comes about easily. As soon as they are through the breakwater, he heads across to the western side of Limon Bay. There are few lights on this side of the bay and before he gets too close, he brings the schooner into the wind and goes forward and drops the anchor.

Harry follows him. "What are you doing? Colón is on the other side of the bay." Jamie lowers the sails and uses the halyard on the foresail to put the dinghy over the side. Harry looks at the dinghy. "I'm not going ashore here. There's nothing here."

"Harry, get in the dinghy."

"You can't just leave me out here. I'm on your crew list."

"Not anymore. You're jumping ship. Claire, go get his bag. I think it's already packed." They wait as Claire drags Harry's bag up on deck and gives it to Jamie. Jamie drops it in the dinghy. "Get in Harry."

"Look, we're kind of friends. I gave you free beer."

"It wasn't your beer. Get in the dinghy, Harry, or you'll have to swim ashore."

Harry climbs in the dinghy and Jamie follows him. "You row." Harry rows and Jamie guides him over to Shelter Bay. When the dinghy scrapes the bottom, Harry grabs his bag and walks into the night. No good-bye. Jamie rows back to the schooner.

Claire meets him as he climbs aboard. "What do we do now?"

"We anchor on the other side." He starts the engine and raises the anchor to the surface and heads across the bay to The Flats. He drops the anchor near the yacht club, just outside the other boats.

"Should I go ashore now?"

"We wait until it's light and then I'll clear with the port authorities."

He goes below to the galley and makes coffee. He takes two cups to the aft cabin and gives one to Claire. "I'll see if I can get you on another boat that's ready to transit the canal. It will be at least a few days or more before I can get the schooner through. The canal is a busy place."

"Why don't I just take a bus or train to the other side of the canal?"

"Doyle put Harry on us, so Doyle is probably here too. He'll be watching for you."

"Why are you helping me?"

"I said I would take you San Francisco."

"That's not a reason."

She is smiling, waiting. "Alright, because you smell good."

"I like that reason."

As soon as it's light Jamie gets out the binoculars and surveys the boats in the harbor. He recognizes a sloop. *Sundowner*. Keppler is on deck. He goes below to Claire. "I'm going to row over to a yacht and talk to the skipper. In the meantime, pack everything you have in a seabag and be ready to leave. Don't leave any of your things behind. I may get searched at some point."

He rows over to *Sundowner* and hails the boat. Keppler looks up. "Jamie, it's been a while. Come aboard." They catch up on what has happened since Penang. Debora and Keppler's wife left *Sundowner* in India. "My wife got sick and wanted to go home and Debora went with her. I had a hard time getting a crew in India. It was even worse in Egypt and I ended up sailing single-handed to Cyprus. Thank god I found Jim and Mary Major in Gibraltar. They're a good crew."

"When do you transit the canal?"

"In a couple of days. I'm looking for a fourth linehandler."

"I'd like to help you out but I've got to keep an eye on the schooner . . . I've got someone on board who wants to get to Balboa as soon as possible."

Keppler points to a sloop close-by. "That German boat *Frieda* is looking for someone. They're leaving tomorrow morning."

"Can you introduce me to them?"

"I'll tell you what. I'll bring them over to the schooner this afternoon. I'm sure they'll want to have a look at her."

In the afternoon they row over in two dinghies, Keppler, the two Majors, and Fritz and Frieda. Jamie shows them around the schooner and when they all gather in the main cabin, he breaks out a bottle of rum. They drink it with lime and water until late in the afternoon and since Fritz is leaving at five the next morning, Jamie arranges for Claire to go over to *Frieda* and sleep there.

Claire kisses him before she gets into *Frieda's* dinghy. "I'll see you in Balboa?"

"If you wait for me. It may be a week or so before I can get there."

"I'll find some way to wait."

Fritz is a little drunk, complaining about his time in Cuba, so when they get in his dinghy, Frieda rows. Fritz shouts up to Jamie. "Don't go to Cuba. Nothing is ever made there."

Jamie gets up before dawn and watches *Frieda* leave. Keppler is on board, raising *Frieda's* anchor. He doesn't see Claire in the early light. He told her to stay below until later. The sloop moves off with her running lights on, heading for the locks. The pilot boat approaches and the pilot steps aboard.

Later in the morning Jamie rows over to the yacht club and takes a taxi to the port authorities for his clearance. He has his and Harry's passport. Claire isn't on his crew list. The taxi driver takes him to Western Union and he wires his uncle to send him some money to transit the canal. The earliest date the canal authorities can give him is in four days. He goes back to the yacht club and orders a sandwich and a beer.

He watches for Doyle and then sees him arriving in a taxi wearing the same Hawaiian shirt and a new Panama to cover his sunburnt head. "I saw your boat in the bay." He looks around the club. "Where's Harry?"

"I don't know but if you see him you can give him this." He hands him Harry's passport.

Doyle sits at the table opposite Jamie and looks at the passport. "What do you mean you don't know? Is he in town? The place is filthy."

"Harry jumped ship."

Doyle stares at him. "What kinda game are you playin'?"

"What kind are you playing?"

"Look, let me tell you something. Meyers is dead. They aren't sure about the cause but it happened too fast. If you ask me I think the girl helped him along. So now she's up to her neck in some deep shit. So tell me where she is? Is she on your boat?"

"What's her name?"

Doyle raises his eyebrows. "I don't give out that kinda information."

"Is that how it is?"

"That's how it is."

"Good, then we're even."

Doyle stands up. "I've had enough of this." He puts his hands on the table and leans in toward Jamie. "You think you're smart but I'll get the girl yet."

Jamie raises his glass. "The beer's good. The sandwiches are pretty decent, too."

When his uncle's money arrives, Jamie buys four three-inch manila ropes one-hundred-and-twenty-five feet long. He asks around the yacht club and hires three local Americans to help him handle the lines in the canal locks. In the morning a boat brings the linehandlers out to the schooner and Jamie raises the anchor and cats it. As he heads for the locks, he picks up the pilot who takes the helm and guides the schooner into the first lock behind a Greek freighter. The men on the edge of the canal throw down lines and Jamie and the three line-handlers tie the ropes Jamie bought to the lines and the men haul the ropes up to the top of the canal and attach them to the mules, engines that run on tracks. As water floods into the lock and the schooner rises, the four mules keep the schooner in the center of the lock.

Three locks raise them up and then the pilot heads the schooner out on Gatun Lake. After being at sea, crossing the calm lake has an eerie feeling, especially with the green jungle on both sides. At lunch Jamie hands out bowls of bean and cornbread and a bucket of ice with cans of coke in it. The line-handles sit on the cabin top and watch the jungle slide past and Jamie takes the helm to relieve the pilot. In the afternoon they reach the Gaillard Cut, an artificial valley carved through the Continental Divide, and then another three locks lowers them to Pacific side of Panama. Jamie powers the schooner out of the last lock and the sun goes down and it quickly turns dark. A boat picks up the line-handles and the pilot boat picks up the pilot. Jamie passes under the Bridge of the Americas and moves out of the ship channel to where the boats are anchored off the Pacific Yacht Club. He puts the engine in neutral and drops the anchor and immediately a Canal Zone Police boat comes along side and three officers and Doyle step aboard.

Doyle grins. "I said I would get the girl."

Stella Maris

Jamie points at Doyle. "He's not an officer. I don't want him on board."

The sergeant tells Doyle to step back on the police boat and then turns to Jamie. "We have a search warrant. Is there anyone else on board?"

"No. What are you searching for?"

"We are looking for a woman name Claire Meyers."

"I just finished transiting the canal. Do you mind if I go below and make some coffee?" The sergeant waves him below. He makes a pot of coffee and takes it and four cups and sits at the table in the main cabin. The officers come in after searching and Jamie pours them each a cup of coffee. "Her name isn't Meyers. She isn't any relation to Morris Meyers. Did Doyle tell you that?"

"Mr. Doyle urged us to stop you as soon as you exited the canal. He claims you would leave as soon as possible."

"I can't leave. I don't have a crew. And you know that as a private detective Doyle isn't interested in law enforcement. He is just using you guys to help him recover the money Morris Meyers stole. I don't see how this is a situation for the police."

"Mr. Doyle presented this as a special situation involving theft from an American institution. As Canal

Zone Police we have considerable discretion in how we use our authority."

"You didn't find anyone on board, so are we finished here?"

The sargeant puts down his cup. "Okay. It's Friday night. Come to my office on Monday morning and you can sign a statement." He stands up. "The Canal Zone is directly under the federal government, so we don't want some rich American complaining to his congressman that we sat on our hands with this." The three policemen climb on deck and the police boat comes along side and picks them up. Jamie watches the boat's lights until they disappear in the flare on the waterfront. He goes forward and rigs his riding light.

Jamie puts the dinghy over the side and rows among the anchored boats, looking for *Frieda*. He sees a cabin light and recognizes the sloop. He rows over and knocks on the hull. Claire appears in the cockpit.

"Jamie, come aboard. No one is here."

Jamie ties the dinghy to a lifeline stanchion and climbs aboard. "Where is Fritz and Frieda?"

She hugs him and they kiss. "They are in town. Come below."

Stella Maris

In the saloon Claire looks at Jamie and then turns off the cabin light. They quickly undress and lie on the settee. "I've been waiting for you."

Jamie leaves Claire on *Frieda* until Fritz and Frieda return the next day. That night Jamie picks her up and rows her to the schooner.

"There's just the two of us. It will be a lot of work."

"I don't care. I want to leave."

He hoists the dinghy on board and starts the engine and gives Claire a course to steer while he gets the anchor on board and lashed down. He goes aft and stands next to her at the helm. Navigation lights and ship's lights dot the night and they pass among them as they head south. When they have cleared the harbor area, Jamie turns off the engine. "We have to sail. We don't have much fuel."

Claire helps him raise the mainsail and then he raises the foresail and the headsails. The wind is light and variable and as the schooner rolls gently in the sea, the reef points patter on the sails. Claire takes the helm as Jamie goes below to make coffee. He brings two cups aft to the helm. Claire takes a sip and then looks at her palm. "Do you think I'll get calluses on my hands like yours?"

"No, your calluses will be much nicer They'll be envy of the whole yachting world."

"Sometime you talk such nonsense. Why are we heading south. I though we wanted to go north."

"We have to get out of the Gulf of Panama and round Point Mala first. Then we head northwest, if the wind lets us."

The sails fill and collapse in the fluky wind. Jamie shows Claire how to work the jib sheet when the wind changes. He goes below and heats up a can of chicken soup and brings a cup to Claire. They sit together, shoulder to shoulder at the helm, not talking. Astern the lights of Panama City grow dim and at midnight Claire goes below and Jamie tries to keep the sails full as the schooner heads out of the Gulf. At dawn the sun lights up the clouds in the east and the wind comes up from the northwest. Jamie tacks the schooner away from the land, leaving Point Mala astern. When Claire climbs on deck, he goes forward to make coffee. He brings two cups and the pot aft to the helm. She drinks her coffee with both hands and Jamie takes the helm.

"We're still heading south."

"The wind is from the northwest. If it holds we'll tack toward the land before noon."

"So we won't be sailing in a straight line."

"No, not unless we get a land breeze."

Jamie takes the cups and the pot below and then takes the light-weather sails out of the locker over the galley. He stores them in the fo'c'sle and carries up the storm trysail and puts it in the locker. He goes back to the fo'c'sle and gets the covers for the fo'c'sle hatch and main skylight and puts them in the locker as well. He expects gale-force winds further up the coast, winds that funnel out of the mountain passes in the northeast. Before noon the wind dies and the schooner drifts northwest with the current. Jamie takes the noon sight. In the afternoon the wind comes off the land from the west and they are able to head the schooner more to the north on the starboard tact. At night the wind fails and veers to the south and then at dawn it dies altogether. Jamie cooks pancakes and eggs for breakfast, takes a morning sun sight and calculates their position. He goes on deck, gets out the bucket and strips off his shirt and shorts.

"Are you going to put on a show?"

"I'm going to take a saltwater shower. You're next, so get ready." He dumps a bucket of saltwater over his head and uses a bar of saltwater soap he bought in Colón to lather up and then he dumps two more bucket over his head.

"Come on, it's your turn."

She stands up but doesn't undress. "These clothes need to be washed anyway."

"It's easier to wash them if you take them off." She hesitates and then turns her back and undresses. Jamie has a bucket of water ready and he dumps it over her head and she screams.

"What's the matter? The water isn't that cold."

"No, but it's not hot either." He soaps her back and then hands her the soap and goes below for towels. When he comes back she is lathered up and he dumps a couple of buckets of water over her and hands her a towel.

"The trick with saltwater showers is to dry off completely so the salt doesn't stick to your skin." He dries her back and then begins rubbing her hair. "Especially the hair." She goes below and he dumps their clothes in a bucket of water and scrubs them and wrings them out. He hangs the clothes from the ratlines in the main shrouds and when Claire comes on deck she looks at the clothes drooping in the windless air.

"You did our laundry?"

"Of course." He points. "Those are the flags of our domesticity."

She laughs. "I like that you do the housework."

With the wind from the northwest and the west and something with no wind, they slowly make their way up the coast of Panama and then Costa Rica and into the Gulf of Papagayo. In the late afternoon Jamie is below when a strong gust of wind hits the schooner. The *Sailing Directions* suggests to stay close to land during a Papagayo, as the winds are stronger farther out at sea. They are just a few miles off the coast and sailing away from the land on the starboard tack when the schooner began to heel over and race through a calm water of the Gulf. The wind surprises Claire and she yells from the helm. Jamie runs on deck, releases the main sheet and runs forward and releases the peak halyard, scandalizing the mainsail. He lowers the throat halyard and then holding the toping lift he yells at Claire to haul in the mainsheet. As the main boom swings over the gallows he drops it in place. "Make the sheet fast and keep the helm to windward." He runs forward and lowers the jib and makes it fast to the samson post. He unhanked the jib from the headstay earlier so he doesn't have to go out on the bowsprit to handle it. The schooner heaves-to under foresail and staysail. Jamie faces the wind for a moment and then decides to set the storm trysail and take down the foresail. The schooner rides easy under the trysail, heeling over with her lee rail almost in the water.

He goes aft to Claire. "You did well with the main sheet. You make a good crew."

She smiles. "What do we do now?"

"We go below and sleep."

They crawl into the lee bunk. Claire falls asleep and Jamie hugs her as the schooner slowly drifts out to sea. They sleep through the night and at dawn Jamie climbs on deck. The schooner is pointing toward the land with a light wind from the south. He lowers the trysail and sets the mainsail and then the foresail and jib. When the schooner picks up speed he tacks and they sail slowly up the coast.

Claire comes on deck and looks at the sails. "I'm beginning to learn some of the sounds this boat makes. That pounding on the deck means she is coming about."

"How did you like the sound of the wind in the rigging last night."

"It was better than any sleeping pill I've ever had."

"You didn't mind me waking you up?"

"No, I went right back to sleep afterwards. There's something about the sea that makes everything more satisfying, especially eating, sleeping, and loving. Don't you think so?"

He smiles and goes below to cook breakfast.

Stella Maris

The wind comes mainly from the northwest, making them tack toward land and then out to sea again. Six days later off the Gulf of Tehuantepec another gale-force wind funnels through a mountain pass and hits the schooner while she is off the coast. Jamie lowers the mainsail and as he is pulling the storm trysail out of the sail locker, the clew on the jib rips out and the sail flaps wildly. Jamie sets the storm trysail and lowers the foresail before taking in the jib. He lowers the jib halyard and climbs out on the bowsprit. The bow dips into the sea and waves wash across the bowsprit. He holds on to the headstay and unfastens the tack of the jib and then slowly makes his way back to the deck. He drags the jib aft and dumps it down the midship hatch. He looks aft. Claire is clinging to the wheel with an uncertain look on her face. The Tehuantepecer is stronger than the last storm. He helps her into the aft cabin and then he stands in the companionway and watches the schooner. The wind blows the bow off to leeward but the schooner righten herself and pitches into sea. He goes below and checks the bilge. There's some water sloshing about and he remembers that he hasn't put on the hatch covers. He climbs on deck and gets the covers from the sail locker. The schooner's lee rail is in the water and the foredeck is taking water over the bow.

He goes to the foremast and ties the end of the staysail halyard around his waist before putting the cover over the fo'c'sle hatch. He turns the ventilator to face leeward and crawls to the main skylight and puts the cover over it. He doesn't want to turn the engine on, so he uses the hand pump to empty the bilge.

In the aft cabin Claire is sitting on the lee bunk. "This is worse than the last one, isn't it?"

"It just means we'll drift more to the southwest."

"What if it gets stronger?"

He sits next to her and put an arm around her. "I don't think it will. It's not a tropical storm."

Jamie sits in the main cabin on the lee settee as the gale continues to blow from the northeast. The jib is on the table and he's sewing the clew. When he is done he holds up the the corner of the sail to the skylight. It's temporary but it should hold until Acapulco. He climbs on deck and walks on the windward side, checking first the staysail and then going aft and checking the trysail. The main sheet has been washed overboard and is trailing aft. He starts hauling it back on board and he sees a mahi-mahi swimming in the shadow of the schooner's transom. He goes in the chartroom and gets out a fishing line with a feathered lure and lets it out over the stern. The mahi-mahi strikes the lure almost immediately and Jamie hauls the fish up and drops it in the steering well and takes the hook out of its mouth. The mahi-mahi begins to lose its coloring as he carries it and a bucket to the foredeck and cuts out fillets from both sides with his rigging knife and throws the carcass overboard. He takes the bucket to the galley and dumps the fillets in the sink and goes back to wash off the deck.

He dices one fillet and marinates the pieces, covering them with lime and onion and a little salt. No refrigeration, no ice. It doesn't matter. He waits an hour and then eats a plate of the fish with salted crackers. He takes a second plate to Claire in the aft cabin. She's awake, sitting up in her bunk.

"I brought you something to eat."

She looks at the plate. "What is it?"

"I just caught a mahi-mahi."

"It doesn't look cooked."

"It's not cooked. It's ceviche. It's marinated. Try some." He puts a little ceviche on a cracker and hands it to her. She's reluctant but she puts it in her mouth and eats.

Her eyes brighten up. "It's good. Give me the plate."

"I'll fry up some fillets with boiled potatoes later."

"You can make some more of this."

"We're out of lime. We'll get some more in Acapulco."

A molten sun hangs above the clouds in the west as the schooner moves slowly through the ocean swell on a close reach. Porpoise swim through the dark blue water, pacing the schooner as they dive under her bow and then come up again and blow. Jamie sits next to Claire at the helm and smiles at her. "What do you think of all this? The sun and the sky and the sea?"

"It's beautiful." She looks forward. "The porpoise too. I wish it was always like this."

As the sun sinks, the clouds begin to turn red. "It often is."

"I don't think the storms were beautiful but now that they are behind us they don't seem so bad. Maybe I'll make a real sailor yet."

Her blond hair is tied back and she has a slight sunburn on her cheek. When she turns toward him, her eyes are the dark blue of the sea. "I couldn't find a better crew." He looks to the west. "Red sky at night. I'll go fry the fish we caught." He stands and starts forward before turning back to her. "You eat like a real sailor."

Stella Maris

As they sail up the Mexican coast, haze hides the land but it's not far away and when the sun sinks below the horizon and the east turns dark, Jamie sees the Acapulco light flashing. The schooner is making five knots on the port tack and he sails toward the light until they are a few miles out and heaves-to under main and staysail. Claire is sleeping below and he sits at the helm, waiting for dawn.

He makes coffee and puts the schooner back on the course and heads into Acapulco Bay. Claire comes on deck and takes the helm. As Roqueta Island comes abeam he turns on the engine and takes down the sails and then he rigs the anchor readying to drop. He stands beside Claire and guides her as she slowly steers around the peninsula that protects the yacht harbor at the western end of the bay. They stay outside the other boats and anchor with enough room for the schooner to swing.

Port officials come aboard and Jamie takes them down to the main cabin and passes out cigarettes and offers a bottle of rum. He smiles as much as possible and waits until the head official gives him a clearance for all of Mexico. He sees the port officials off and heads for the aft cabin. Claire is sitting on her bunk. "Let me show you something." She pulls up the foot of the mattress and lifts out a bag and spreads jewelry on the bunk. Necklaces, bracelets, earrings and brooches. The gold is a dull color in the dim cabin light.

"It looks old. What is it?"

"Pre-Columbian jewelry."

"How did you get it on board? You brought it out in a boat in Bonaire?"

"I used your dinghy."

"What are you going to do with it?"

"If I return it to the museum they'll give me a finder's fee."

"How do you contact them? Did you work at the museum?"

She looks at him without smiling. "Are you going to grill me?"

"This changes things. I want to know where I stand."

"Where you stand? We just spent three weeks together. Nothing has changed."

"Okay, let's go to the yacht club and take a shower."

That evening she tells Jamie to put on trousers and a shirt. She wants to go into town. They take a taxi and drive along the waterfront where street lights and go-go club marquees brighten the night. There are crowds of young Americans in front of the go-go clubs and Claire tells the taxi driver to stop. "Come on, Jamie. Let's go dance." They walk into a club to the sound of go-go music. The women dancing on the stage throw their elbows right and left and the couples on the dance floor imitate them. He buys two drinks, white rum with pineapple, and when he won't dance, Claire goes out on the dance floor alone. He watches her until a college kid comes up to him.

"Nice tan, man. Are you here on spring break?"
"No. My break is a little longer."
"Cool. You mind if I dance with your girlfriend."
"I think she's looking for someone to dance with."

The college kid walks on the dance floor and starts talking to Claire. He too young for her but she dances with him anyway. Jamie sits at an empty table and drinks his rum and when he's finished he drinks Claire's rum. His mind wonders to the sound of *California Dreamin'.* The air is thick and hot. He goes outside and stands in the night breathing in the harbor smells of seaweed and fish. Claire comes out of the club with a crowd around her. "Come on, Jamie. We're going to another club." He follows them for a while and when they reach the next club he turns around and walks slowly back to the yacht club.

Claire goes to Mexico City. While she's gone Jamie gets the schooner ready to head north, taking on fuel, water and food. He has a sailmaker repair the clew on the jib and then he decides to take the sheets and towels to a laundry. He pulls Claire's bunk apart and finds a golden bracelet. He takes it over to the light and examines it. It's a museum replica of a pre-Columbia bracelet he saw on her bunk. Was she at the museum? Did she work there? He knew she was involved with Davenport but he doesn't know how much. It doesn't seems to matter now.

Two weeks later he's handed a note at the yacht club. *I'm at the Buenavista, room 415, Claire.* He walks up the hill and into the hotel lobby and looks around. He should have changed his clothes. Claire opens the door of her room. She is smiling and her blond hair is loose, hanging down over the collar of the hotel bathrobe. She leads him to the balcony where the view looks out over the cliffs to the Pacific Ocean. The table on the balcony is covered with food.

"Have lunch with me. There's enough for both of us." They sit at the table.

"You sold the gold jewelry."

"Yes, I was very lucky and now we don't have to worry about anything." She stops eating. "Isn't it terrific here? We get a view of the ocean and fresh fruit and fresh bread delivered to the room. God, how I missed fresh bread."

"You're going to stay here."

"We are both going to stay here. I registered the room in both our names." She looks at him and her voice changes. "Sailing up from Panama was a real adventure but I'm tired of saltwater showers and long dull watches at the helm and I think the sea air is bad for my skin." She stands and walks to balcony and looks out on the sea. "This is the real life."

"This? This is a postcard life."

"Well, It's the life I want."

"The schooner is a real life."

"We aren't talking about the same thing."

"But we are. We're talking about us and you're saying there'no longer is an us. There's no us without the schooner and the sea. Don't you see that the schooner makes you a better person because there's no place on her for lying and stealing." He looks down at the plate in front of him. Butter for the bread and mayonnaise for the shrimp. After being at sea the food is too rich for him. "I thought the schooner changed you."

She looks out at the ocean. "Jamie, I like you. I like you a lot and I want you to stay here with me." She turns back. "You're a little naive but tender and loyal. I don't think I could ever find anyone else like you."

He stands up and moves away from the table. "You're wrong. The sea air makes your skin glow." He walks to the door of the room.

"Jamie, wait. Are you leaving?"

"I'm taking the schooner to San Francisco. It's what I've been doing all along. You know that."

"Will you come back then, after you reach San Francisco?

"Good-bye, Claire.

Jamie asks around the yacht harbor but nobody wants to go north with him on the schooner. He rows over to the yacht club and pays his bill and sits at a table drinking a last beer and looking at the boats preparing to sail to the South Seas. He'll sail there too, someday. He looks up at the hill but he can't see her hotel. Of course he knew as soon as he saw the gold lying on the bunk that it would come to this. She used him but he doesn't mind that, he even put himself up to be used. What he minds is that she misled him about her love for the sea. She fooled him and then she called him naive.

In the morning he starts the engine and raises the anchor. He moves out to the middle of Acapulco Bay and hauls his anchor on deck and lashes it down. When he clears Roqueta Island he sets the sails. He has to work hard to sweat the sag out of the mainsail. He hardens in the sheets and heads the schooner away from the land. He looks back at her hotel, a white building sitting on the cliffs, rooms with a view of the ocean. He looks forward again. The horizon is a sharp line between the pale sky and the dark sea. White caps slide toward the schooner and a few of them reach her and wash against her bow. The bow dips into a trough between the waves and he can see the ocean spread out before him. It's much more than just a view.

Milton Keynes UK
Ingram Content Group UK Ltd.
UKHW010821220424
441551UK00005B/401